LOVE THE WAY YOU ARE

Winter Lake

RHIAN CAHILL

Rhian Cahill

Love The Way You Are
Winter Lake
By Rhian Cahill

Love Me Like You Do
Love The Way You Are
When You Love Someone
Let Me Love You
Wild Rush Of Love

LOVE THE WAY YOU ARE
WINTER LAKE BOOK 2

Who needs 20/20 vision to find true love?

There's something familiar about the gorgeous woman across the crowded club. When he "accidentally" bumps into her, Alex Dean is shocked to discover what it is. The tall, leggy blonde is none other than Sadie Emerson, his college math tutor—and the subject of more fantasies than he could count. Years later, she's looking better than ever. He has to have her. Tonight.

Does it really matter that she thinks she's going home with his buddy, Alec Dane?

Apparently it does because she sneaks away the morning after. *Twice.* First, when she discovers her mistake, then when she decides her upcoming move to Winter Lake makes them a two-day stand at best. But the sex is off-the-charts combustible, and Alex is already seeing stars, hearing bells...envisioning houses and picket fences and other things he'd never considered.

Now all he has to do is convince Sadie his feelings are real. His shy wallflower might consider him a mistake—but Alex has never been more certain.

Mr.C.
You're every breath I take.

CHAPTER 1

"C'MON. DON'T BE A CHICKEN." Mel took a sip of her margarita. "I thought this was the beginning of the new Sadie—"

"Dee," she corrected.

"What?"

"The new me is Dee not Sadie." A new name, a new woman. Or at least that was the plan.

Shame the name change hadn't boosted her confidence. It seemed she was still the same nerdy wallflower she'd always been—too shy to say hello to the hot guy across the room.

Mel waved her hand, her drink sloshing up the sides of her glass. "Sadie, Dee, whatever. Just go over there and say hi."

"You only want me to go so you can have a shot with one of the other guys."

"Well duh! Have you seen them?" Mel downed the rest

of her cocktail then fanned her face. "That's some seriously smokin'-hot man perfection over there."

Sadie sighed. Dammit. She couldn't even think of herself as Dee. So much for reinventing herself.

She glanced over Mel's shoulder at the group of men on the far side of the dimly lit club and murmured, "Comes with their profession I guess." Her eyes snagged on one man in particular. Tall, dark, and every woman's wet dream.

"What?" Mel leaned closer, hand cupping her ear. "You'll have to speak up, the music's loud in here."

Her friend wasn't wrong. Sadie's ears were ringing, and the thumping beat vibrated up through her feet and rattled her bones. She was pretty sure they could hear the music two counties over. "Never mind."

Mel reached for the pitcher and topped off her glass. Sadie quickly placed her hand over her own empty glass to stop Mel from getting her any more drunk than she was. Already she feared she was in for one hell of a hangover.

"I'm good."

"If you were, you'd go over there. You're not drunk enough if you're still sitting here with me." Mel attempted to kick her under the table—the six inch stiletto her friend wore barely skimmed Sadie's leg—and almost toppled off her chair.

Laughing, Sadie righted her. "Watch it."

Swaying a little, Mel gripped the edge of the table with both hands to steady herself. "Like you, I'm good."

Sadie arched an eyebrow. "Really?"

"No. Actually, I'm not. I need a strong, strapping hunk of man to take my drunk ass home, where he'll take complete advantage of my intoxicated state and deliver me to the stars."

"There's just one flaw in your plan."

"Yeah, I know." Mel sighed. Exaggerated a pout. "My best friend won't introduce me to the man in question."

Sadie laughed. "Besides that."

"Oh, you're just a ray of sunshine raining all over my parade tonight."

"You won't remember any of it come morning."

"With any luck I'll still be coming in the morning."

Sadie shook her head. After six years, she was still amazed by her friendship with Mel. They were opposites in every way. Mel was outgoing and the life of the party, while Sadie preferred to skip the party altogether. "Why are we friends again?"

"Because you need me to push you out of your shell. Force you to be social." Mel stood on wobbly legs and tried to drag Sadie out of her seat. "Now get over there so we can both get lucky."

"Fine." Sadie allowed herself to be pushed to her feet. "But I'm going to the bathroom first. These stupid contacts are killing me. I can't believe I let you talk me into getting them." The smoky air of the club had gotten in her eyes and dried them out. Not only did they hurt but she couldn't see clearly either.

"Excellent." Mel flopped back into her chair. "I'll wait here for my knight in shining armor."

Sadie watched Mel gulp the remainder of her margarita and top up her glass again. "You might want to slow down or you'll pass out before your knight arrives."

Her friend frowned at her drink. "Good point." She pushed the full glass across the table to Sadie. "You drink it."

She turned away but Mel grabbed her arm and spun her back.

"What have you got to lose? This time next week you'll be in Winter Lake, New York. At best you'll have a hot one-night-stand memory to take with you. At worst a bad one or none at all. Either way, you'll never have to see the guy again."

"But—"

Mel gave her arm a shake. "No. No buts. You can do this. You *need* to do this. Cut loose, Sadie. Be daring. For once, take life by the throat and give it a shake, go after what you want."

She was already doing that by walking away from the only life she'd ever known in the city to do what she'd always dreamed of doing. Live in a small town where she knew her neighbors and her life didn't make her head spin.

If she could find the courage to do that, she could manage a little more to take her across the room to say high to her college crush, right?

"You can do it," Mel encouraged.

Nodding, Sadie broke free of Mel's hold. "You're right. Dee Emerson, CFO of the Economic Development Board of Winter Lake, wouldn't blink at going over there." She *could* be Dee. She *needed* to be Dee. Her dream future depended on it.

"No, she wouldn't." Mel's lips curled in a smug smile. "Now drink that glass of courage."

Doing something she never did, Sadie picked up the margarita and drained it in one go.

She shuddered as the cold liquid slid down her throat, through her chest, and into her stomach, where it hit the pool of alcohol already in her belly.

Setting the empty glass down, she took a deep breath and turned to look at the group of men fifty feet away.

Her vision was blurred due to the new contacts irritating her eyes but she could still see—if a little fuzzily—Alec Dane and his group of friends with their usual entourage of women. She had tutored most of the guys in college—knew them by name; she shouldn't be afraid to go over there and say hello.

Sadie straightened her shoulders.

She *wouldn't* be afraid. Not tonight.

She'd go to the bathroom and remove the contacts then she'd wander past and pretend to notice them for the first time. Then she'd smile and talk like any other sexy, confident twenty-six-year-old, and maybe, just maybe, Sadie would get to live out her ultimate fantasy.

One night with Alec Dane.

CHAPTER 2

ALEX DEAN WATCHED the blonde he'd had his eye on all night weave her way through the crowd toward the bathrooms. Putting his beer down, he walked away from the redhead who'd been giving him the come-on for the better part of an hour without a backward glance.

He'd made it clear he wasn't interested except Red was either too drunk to register his brush-off or figured she could change his mind.

She might have had a chance if he hadn't already spotted the blonde.

Red wasn't the first to mistake him for his friend Alec Dane. Not only did they share a similar name, but they looked so alike they could pass for brothers, and during their rowdy college days, had on more than one occasion.

He kept his eye on the back of the blonde's head as he followed her through the crush of bodies. She was tall—

taller than his usual type, anyway—so it wasn't hard to keep her in sight.

Something about her had struck a chord the second he'd laid eyes on her. He'd been staring at her for a good portion of the night and he still couldn't work out what it was that held him enthralled.

She disappeared into the women's restroom and he glanced around for a spot to wait. A small section of wall tucked around the corner from the club's main room formed an out-of-the-way alcove and the shadows meant he could watch her unseen when she finally emerged. Get a gauge of what it was—other than her being a knockout—that had his insides tight and his cock stretching to full length.

He settled in for the long haul—in his experience, women took forever in the bathroom—but it was only a couple of minutes before she stepped back into the hall.

She propped the door open for another woman to pass through and the bright light from inside gave him a clear view of her face.

Alex pushed off the wall.

Sadie Emerson.

No wonder he'd been captivated. Alex hadn't seen her in three—no—four years.

She'd been the football team's math tutor his senior year of college and he'd had all sorts of fantasies woven around the studious sexy glasses wearing Sadie Emerson. And in his opinion, she'd only gotten hotter.

Before she could pass him, he moved into her path. "Hey."

"Oh." She pressed a hand to her chest. Took a half-step back. "Sorry. I didn't see you."

"My fault." He smiled down at her. Estimated she was around four inches short of his six-two.

"Alec?" She squinted, leaned closer and peered up at him. "Alec Dane?"

Alex's gut cramped. "Ah…"

"Wow. I haven't seen you in years. How have you been?"

He'd never objected to being mistaken for his friend before, but there was no ignoring the ball of acid currently burning a hole in his stomach. He couldn't say why he didn't correct her though.

"I'm good. How have you been?"

"Great. I'm great." She smiled.

They stared at each other for long seconds.

"Well. I, um, should get back," she said, indicating the noisy club behind him.

He stepped to the side and blocked her when she went to move around him. "Can I buy you a drink?"

"Oh." She licked her lips. Looked away. Glanced back. "Y-yes. Sure."

Alex put his hand on her lower back and steered her out of the hallway. Bending down, he brought his mouth close to her ear and pointed to the far end of the bar near the entrance to the club. Away from his friends—from hers. "Let's go over there."

Sadie nodded and headed in that direction.

The crowd thinned the farther away from the dance floor they went. He could have backed off, given her more room, but he liked the feel of her in front of him. The way his chest brushed her back, her ass against his groin every few steps. The scent of her hair as it floated around him—the heat of her so close.

Fantasies stored in the back of his mind came rushing forward. Lust-infused blood pounded in his veins and drummed in his ears, throbbed in his balls. His cock hardened, pressing against the fly of his jeans, the thick denim a rough caress over his bare shaft.

"This okay?" Sadie stopped at the end of the bar.

"Perfect." He leaned into the bar and angled his hips to hide his hard-on. Now they were here, Alex had no idea what to say to her. Glancing away, he tried to get the barman's attention.

"So...do you come here often?"

Alex turned back to Sadie. "No." He'd never been in this club before. It hadn't been around when he'd lived in the city for the four years he was in college.

"This is my first time." She looked around them. "Not sure it's really my thing."

"Oh? What made you come tonight?" He leaned closer so he could hear her over the music and her scent surrounded him. Filled him.

Her mouth kicked up in a half smile and Alex's gaze was drawn to her lips. They glistened under the bar lights but it wasn't gloss. She must have licked them recently. The thought almost made him miss her next words.

"My best friend. She can be pretty persuasive."

"Is that a good or bad thing?"

Sadie laughed, the sound a deep throaty rumble that

came from true humor, not the fake kind Red had been dropping earlier. "Both?"

He couldn't tear his gaze from her mouth. Her lips were full, but not that bee-stung look a lot of women went for. Sadie's didn't appear medically enhanced at all and he wondered how soft they'd be, whether they'd open willingly if he pressed his tongue against the seam...

He gave himself a mental shake to clear the X-rated thoughts from his mind. "Ah, one of those friends."

She nodded. "Yep. But she means well."

"Most of them do." Alex noticed a barman working his way toward them. "What will you have?"

"A bottle of water."

Alex arched an eyebrow. "Water?"

"Yeah." She smiled. "I've had one too many margaritas already."

"You're drunk?" She didn't appear intoxicated to him, except he wasn't exactly an expert on Sadie Emerson.

"Let's say a little tipsy and leave it at that."

He moved closer and before he could engage his brain, lust was taking over and words were pouring out his mouth. "So I could take advantage of your *tipsy* state and steal a kiss?"

His eyes tracked the movement of her tongue as she licked her lips. Fire and need shot through his groin.

"No need to steal one," she murmured, looking up at him through lowered lashes, the action shy, not practiced.

It was all the invitation he needed. Alex didn't wait for her to say anything else. He reduced the distance between them and pressed his mouth to hers.

He flicked his tongue out and traced her lips before increasing the pressure along the seam like he'd imagined. She opened on a small gasp and he took advantage, thrusting deep to taste her heat, to stroke her tongue with his.

She moaned into his mouth, her arms going around his neck, and he wrapped his arms around her waist, pulled her fully against him.

Pressed together, mouths joined, the club—the music, the people—faded away, leaving nothing but the sweet taste of hot woman and urgent need. Her breasts were crushed between them, her nipples hardening by degrees as the kiss went deeper.

Alex couldn't stop himself from grinding his cock against her. His hips rocked forward and Sadie had to know what he wanted. Where this was leading.

He slid a hand up her spine and gripped the back of her head, tangled his fingers in her hair. With the other, he palmed her ass, pressed her closer.

She melted into him.

A groan rumbled in his chest. They fit in a way that left him reeling. He'd never experienced such intense need from a kiss. He had to have more. More of *her*.

All of her.

Pulling back, he spoke against her lips. "Come home with me."

"Oh..." Her hot breath fanned over his mouth, her eyelids fluttering open to reveal her lust-dazed hazel eyes. "Y-yes."

CHAPTER 3

SADIE DIDN'T KNOW how she'd found the courage to go home with Alec. But she had. And here she was in the foyer of his building, waiting for the elevator.

She'd almost hyperventilated in the cab. But as usual, her best friend picked the perfect moment to encourage her to break out of her shell.

Receiving the message from Mel had been a timely reminder of why she was here. She was taking charge of her life—going after what she wanted. And what she wanted was a night of pleasure with the man standing beside her.

When the elevator arrived, they stepped inside and Alec punched the top button on the control panel. The doors slid closed with a soft whoosh, enclosing them in the small space.

"I'm between places so I'm staying with a friend," he offered.

She wasn't sure why he felt the need to explain his

living arrangements but she added her own. "Me too. I'm sleeping on Mel's couch until I leave next week."

"Leave? Mel?" Alec turned and crowded her into the wall, seeming to take up all available breathing space as he did.

"Um..."

"I'm hoping Mel is short for Melanie or Melissa or some other female's name." He pressed into her, his body hard and hot. "I don't share. And I'm definitely not interested in being the other guy."

"Oh. No. I'm not—"

"Good."

Sadie didn't get a chance to respond before Alec slammed his mouth on hers. He didn't explore like he had at the club. No. This kiss started deep—his tongue thrusting between her lips and demanding instant surrender.

She moaned, the sound swallowed by his mouth. The man knew how to kiss. How to take her from interested to craving with the brush of his tongue. Her fingers flexed, gripped, dug into arms thick with muscle.

Alec palmed her ass. Tugged and lifted until she stood on her toes and his cock pressed into her, right on her clit. Sadie gasped as sensation shot through her.

He pulled free, breathing hard. "Not enough."

The elevated jolted to a stop and he grabbed her hand, his fingers slipping between hers in a natural hold that felt too comfortable for Sadie's peace of mind.

This was sex.

A one-night stand.

No repeat.

She needed to remember that.

Tugging her along the hallway behind him, Alec's long strides ate up the ground one step to her two, making her choice of flats a lucky one.

"Excuse the mess." He unlocked the door and swung it wide. "After you."

Sadie paused just inside. The place was dark and she was afraid to step any farther with her blurred sight. "Light?"

"Don't need one," he said as the door closed with a loud click behind them.

The small amount of light coming in from the hall disappeared. Before she could panic, he grabbed her hand again and pulled her after him.

"This way."

She stuck close. Attempted to follow in his footsteps as he navigated their way through the apartment.

He needn't have worried; without glasses or contacts her vision was limited, and the dark only made it worse, so there was no way she could see the state of the apartment.

Alec pulled her in front of him and began to walk her backward. "Made it."

"What?" She couldn't see clearly. Only shadows in various shades of black—all a little fuzzy.

He moved closer and wrapped his arms around her waist. "Last chance to back out."

"Back out?" Her brain didn't seem to work with him so close. The alcohol in her system probably didn't help but it wasn't enough to impair her decision making. She was fully aware of what she doing, going home with Alec. What she would be doing in a few minutes.

"I'm a straight shooter, Sadie—"

"Dee."

"What?" She felt more than saw him lean away.

"I go by Dee now."

"Why?" One of his hands traveled up her spine to cup the back of her neck, his fingers massaging, and she shivered as warmth soaked through her skin.

"It's b-better than Sadie."

"Hmm..." His lips skimmed her jaw. "I like Sadie. I always did."

"Oh, well, um..."

Alec sucked her earlobe into his mouth, crimped it with his teeth, flicked it with his tongue. "You don't mind if I keep calling you Sadie, right?"

He could call her whatever the hell he wanted as long as he kept up what he was doing. She moaned. "Okay." Was that husky voice hers?

Alec's talented mouth explored her neck. He used his lips, his tongue. His teeth.

Sadie was soon rocking her lower body into his. "Please."

He chuckled. "Oh, don't worry. I aim to please."

Her knees shook when he slipped one hand beneath the front of her top, curved it around her waist, and yanked her closer. There was no missing the hard ridge of his cock digging into her belly.

"I can't get enough of you," he spoke against her shoulder, his marauding mouth having finished with her neck. "I want you naked so I can taste every inch of you."

"Yes." The word hissed through her lips.

He shoved his other hand under her shirt. "Let's get this off for a start."

She raised her arms to help. When her top was over her head and on the floor, she reached for him and said, "You too."

"Definitely." Together they removed his shirt. "The rest," he demanded, tugging at her skirt.

Instead of a mad rush, they took it slow. Hands sweeping over exposed flesh in unhurried glides as they moved on to each item of clothing.

"I can't decide between going slow and racing to the finish," Alec murmured against her cheek. "You make me want it all right now. Except I don't want this to be over either."

Sadie understood what he meant. She wanted it all at once but never wanted the feelings rushing through her to end either. She'd never experienced this level of desire. Things were racing through her mind. Naughty, carnal things she knew nothing about.

Desire and need filled her, making her tremble and sweat, giving her the courage to do what she wanted.

Reaching between them, she wrapped her hand around his cock and gently squeezed, testing his size and shape. His hips bucked, his steely length sliding through her fingers.

"Fuck, that feels good," he groaned, his hips rocking quicker.

It did. The heat. The hardness. The silky-soft skin gliding back and forth in her hand. Everything about the sensation fascinated her. She wasn't inexperienced but she'd only been with one guy, and their sex life, while satisfying, had not been spectacular. And never adventurous.

"Tighter." Alec thrust faster. "Run your thumb over the head."

She did as instructed and found slick moisture seeping from the top. She'd never gone down on a guy. Patrick had never asked and she'd never offered. Never been interested in doing what a lot of her girlfriends talked about.

Until now.

Right now she wanted to drop to her knees and take him to the back of her mouth. She started to sink down, except Alec stopped her before she got anywhere near her target.

"As much as I want what you're thinking about doing, I'm way too close to the edge to make it longer than a second inside that hot mouth of yours." He pulled her back up in front of him. "Maybe later, once I get my fill of another hot place I want to put my cock in."

His words and phrases were ones she wasn't used to hearing, but she couldn't deny they turned her on. They were carnal, filthy, except they didn't make her feel dirty.

They excited her, sent desire rushing through her until she couldn't think of anything but what he'd said. She wanted him to put his cock wherever he wanted.

"I've got so many things I want to do to you. With you." He leaned down, speaking into her ear, his warm breath fluttering over her skin, sending shivers down her spine. "Ready to play, Sadie?"

She shuddered when his lips brushed her cheek. "Please."

His smiling mouth met hers. "I like it when you beg."

Was she begging? She'd never felt this need to take—be taken—with anyone else.

Was it the years of fantasizing from afar?

Was it finally being the woman Alec Dané wanted that ramped up her arousal?

"Alec." His name fell from her lips on a sigh.

He swept her up in his arms and, spinning around, fell backwards.

"Alec!"

Laughing, he held her close. They hit the bed, bouncing once before he rolled them over and trapped her beneath him.

"Now. What was I...oh yeah. I was going to do some pleasing."

He lowered his head and sucked a nipple into his mouth.

CHAPTER 4

ALEX LOVED how responsive Sadie was. She trembled under his touch and he found himself stroking her just to see and feel that delicate shiver move through her.

Her breasts were a nice handful, her nipples puckered tight from the attention he'd given them. Cupping them in his hands, he brushed his thumbs over those sensitive tips and watched her moan and arch into the caress.

"You take my breath." He couldn't remember enjoying giving a woman pleasure the way he was with Sadie.

Everything he did was met with enthusiasm...greed. The brush of his fingers was met with a quiver. The swipe of his tongue garnered a shudder. It didn't matter what part of his body he stroked her with, Sadie reveled in the sensations each touch delivered.

She was a sensual delight he never wanted to give up. "More?" he murmured against the soft skin between her breasts.

"Yes." She arched up, her spine bowing. "Please."

He moved lower on the bed and used his legs to spread hers. "Open up for me, Sadie."

Her legs parted, her knees bent, fell open, and he slipped between them, his shoulders forcing her thighs wider. He ran a finger through her wet pussy. "You're so wet. So hot."

"Alec."

He loved the throaty sound of her voice and wished it were his name on her lips. His name whispered in that tight pleading tone. "I'm right here, Sadie." Blowing a hot breath over her exposed wet folds he watched the delicate flesh quiver, grow wetter.

Regardless of who she thought he was—what she called him—it was *him* driving her out of her mind with pleasure. Alex Dean who was making her moan and gasp. He wouldn't risk her leaving by correcting her now though.

Leaning forward, Alex spread her slick folds with his thumbs and, flattening his tongue, laved her clit. Her hips bucked and he pressed his forearms across the top of her thighs to hold her in place.

Her flavor flooded his mouth. Sharp and sweet, her juices coated his tongue. Her scent surrounded him and he took a deep breath, wanting—needing—to take as much of her inside as he could get.

She moaned and writhed when he got down to serious business.

He used his mouth—his tongue and teeth—to lick and suck and nip. He used his fingers to stroke, to press and probe and fill. Nothing went unattended. No part of her unexplored.

He'd always enjoyed eating pussy. The soft, hot flesh between a woman's legs wasn't just for burying his cock in. Alex loved nothing more than driving a woman mad with his mouth.

Except unlike with all those other women, where he did it fast so he could fuck them, he wanted to keep Sadie on the edge. Wanted to take her to the peak again and again, pulling her back over and over, until she begged him to stop—begged him to make her come.

She was close to that edge now.

Her fingers clawed at his head, her short nails dragging across his scalp with a sting. He wasn't into pain, but that quick bite of it—the desperation of her grasping touch— urged him on. Drove his arousal higher.

He thrust two fingers into her tight channel and sucked her clit between his lips. Using his teeth, he pinched the hard nub, increased the suction, pumped his fingers fast, and sent her flying.

She arched, a cry of pleasure gurgling in her throat as the first contraction had her pussy gripping his fingers. He wanted to feel those muscles clutching his cock.

Now.

He continued to stroke in and out of her pussy, and suck at her pulsing clit while he blindly searched for the condom he'd dropped on the bed earlier. When foil crinkled beneath his fingers, he fisted the packet. Easing back, he brought her down slowly, stayed with her until the final pulse of her release died away.

Hands shaking—along with the rest of him—he pushed to his knees and tore open the condom. Suited up, he leaned forward and positioned himself between her thighs; the hot kiss of her pussy surrounded the tip of his cock, sending a shaft of pleasure into his balls.

"I'm going to fuck you now, Sadie." He brushed his lips over hers. "Hard."

He swallowed her gasp and thrust his tongue into her mouth as he drove his cock into her body.

There was no going slow.

Alex didn't have it in him.

Not with the wet heat of her enclosing his entire length in a tight fist, sucking him deep each time he sank in.

Frenzied.

Desperate.

They were the only words to describe the way he took her. Took them both.

She wasn't the only one on this wild ride.

He'd fucked plenty of girls—women—and nothing in his memory matched this one.

From the way she yielded beneath him to the way she scratched at his back to pull him closer—her heels digging in to his ass urging him deeper.

Everything about Sadie, about being with her, seemed amplified, as if someone had flipped a switch on his nervous system to amp up his receptors.

Sweat coated his back, his face, and his body shuddered with each plunge into her tight wet heat.

"I want you to come on my cock." Needed her to before he succumbed to the boiling lust squeezing his balls, lighting up his spine, threatening to destroy him with each surging plunge into her.

He wanted her with him. Craved the clutch of her orgasm as much as he craved his own.

"C'mon, Sadie. Come with me."

Alex shifted to his knees, gripped the backs of her thighs, and pushed her legs up toward her chest. He increased his pace, making sure he ground the base of his cock on her clit with each downstroke.

She wrapped her hands around his wrists, holding on with nail-biting tightness as he pounded into her.

He couldn't hold out. No matter how much he wanted to, the hot flash of release burned through his groin and exploded from his balls.

Spasm after spasm rocked him as he came, filling the condom with what felt like a gallon of come.

Sadie bucked beneath him and he buried his entire shaft and stayed there as she shattered around him.

With each convulsion her pussy squeezed him, clamped his length in a soaking wet fist, the pleasure of her body's grip on his almost too much to bear. A wave of heat scorched him from tip to root, sending another surge of mind-blowing sensation through him.

His shaking muscles threatened to give out and he lowered her legs to the bed. With the last of his energy, he rolled to the side, taking Sadie with him.

Harsh breathing and the smell of sex filled the air around them. They were coated in sweat, her breasts sticking to his chest in a tacky grip as their lungs labored to breathe.

Alex might not have full brainpower yet but even he wasn't stupid enough to think that what just happened was normal.

She lived up to and beyond any fantasy he'd come up with back in college.

And as soon as he got his breath back, he was going to make another one of those fantasies pale in comparison to the reality of fucking Sadie Emerson.

CHAPTER 5

SADIE ROLLED over and came up against a warm body.

Alec.

She wasn't sure how long she'd slept—a few minutes at most. Her skin was still damp and little pulses of pleasure continued to ripple through her body, the throb more persistent between her legs.

"Mmm...come here." Alec wrapped an arm around her and pulled her on top of him. "Better."

"Alec." She was stretched out along his length, her legs draped either side of his.

Speaking of lengths. He still had a hard-on.

"Sadie." He nuzzled his nose into her hair by her ear. "Mmm...you smell good."

Lord. The man was delusional. She stank of sweat and sex.

"So good I could eat you up." Alec nipped her earlobe. "Oh, wait. I did."

She could hear the grin in his voice and she couldn't help smiling while her body tightened and throbbed with the memory of him *eating her up*.

"As much as I'd like to do that again, I think we'll try something different this time."

"This time?" Sadie tilted her head so she could look at him. Not that she could see very well in the darkness or without her glasses.

"Yeah." He flexed his hips—ground his erection into her sex. "I want to watch you ride me."

"Ride?" She gasped when he gripped her shoulders and pushed until she sat up, straddling his thighs.

"Oh yeah, definitely want you on top this go 'round." He leaned over and pulled open the top drawer of the bedside table. "Just need...aha!" Brandishing a condom between his thumb and index finger, Alec turned back and held it out. "Want to do the honors?"

She'd never fitted one before, Patrick had always dealt with that himself, but she knew the basics; it couldn't be that hard. "Okay."

She tore the packet open and removed the latex disk. Using feel—because she certainly couldn't see with enough detail—she made sure she had the condom the right way before placing it on the tip of Alec's cock, being sure to pinch the top of the latex to leave the gap her sex-ed teacher in high school had instructed was necessary.

Her fingers trembled as she gripped the base of his shaft with one hand to hold it steady while she slowly rolled the protection down his length with the other.

"Ah. Fuck." His words were strained—rough. "You're killing me here."

Sadie yanked her hands away. "I am?"

Alec chuckled. "Not like that." He finished fitting the condom in one sweep of his hand. "Your hands on me are a fantasy come true. One I'm obviously not capable of handling without going off like a pubescent boy having his first sexual encounter."

"Oh." He'd fantasized about her touching him?

"C'mon. Up you go."

He wrapped his large hands around her waist and lifted, pulling her forward until she was suspended over him.

"Take me in," he ordered.

She reached down and grabbed his cock, the slick surface of the condom sliding against her fingers, the sensation different from his naked shaft.

He shuddered beneath her, his erection jerking in her hand, his hips bucking off the bed. "Shit. Don't tease me," he growled.

A thrill raced through her. The knowledge she had the power to test Alec's restraint turned her on. That she had the ability never occurred to her.

Confidence filled her, strengthened her courage, and gave her the boldness necessary to line her body up with his and sink down.

Her muscles clenched, squeezing his cock within her tender walls as she took all of him in one slow slide.

They groaned in unison. Her pussy fluttered, sending waves of pleasure skimming over nerve endings already raw from her recent releases.

The position pressed Alec's shaft against places she couldn't remember being stimulated before, and it took Sadie a moment to work through the onslaught of sensation.

Once she did, she moved. Rocked and rolled her hips. Tightened and released internal muscles with each slide along his length, drawing moans of pleasure from each of them.

His hands gripped her hips, fingertips digging in, and he began to move her up and down.

"Ride me." His voice was hoarse, the rasp a sensory caress that sent a shiver down her spine. Heat curled in her belly.

She'd never had sex in this position but she wasn't an idiot; she understood the basics, and with Alec's help, she soon found a rhythm using her legs to raise and lower herself.

"Yeah. That's it." His breath came in harsh gasps. "Just like that. Mmm...yeah, like that."

She leaned forward and braced her arms; hands on his chest, elbows locked. With the added stability she picked up speed. Surging up and plunging down in ever-faster strokes that had her orgasm rushing toward her.

"Fuck." Alec's hands tightened, his fingers digging in, his hips thrusting up to meet her. "Your pussy is squeezing the come right out of me."

He was picking her up and slamming her down now. She was nothing more than a puppet in his hands as he drove them both screaming toward that ultimate peak.

And scream is exactly what she did when he leaned up

and managed to get his lips around a nipple and sucked it into his mouth. He pulled hard, using his teeth to hold and scrape while his tongue licked.

Heat arrowed in a direct line from the breast in his mouth to her core. It was the spark she needed to take her over the edge.

"*Alec*." His name burst from her throat as every muscle spasmed in a mind-numbing release that exploded deep inside her then bloomed like a flower uncurling for the sun.

"God. Sadie. *Yes*." Alec buried his face between her breasts and shuddered.

He continued to drive up into her until the last wave of pleasure washed through them and Sadie slumped against his chest. She was slick with sweat and boneless with satisfaction.

She'd never come so hard—or so often in one night.

Mel had been right.

She was going to take one hell of a one-night-stand memory with her to Winter Lake.

CHAPTER 6

Alex woke sometime in the wee hours of the morning. He didn't have an alarm clock and he had no clue where his phone was but the sky beyond the window held the faint light of dawn before it broke. He turned his head and studied the woman beside him.

She was on her stomach, her smooth back exposed for his gaze.

Sadie proved to be far more enticing than he'd ever imagined in college, and he couldn't stop himself from trailing his fingertips over that silky expanse of skin.

She shivered, goose bumps rising up in a wave behind his fingers as he raked them from the base of her neck to the sweet little indents at the top of her ass. He toyed there a while. Brushed his fingers back and forth and watched as she squirmed in her sleep.

He smiled when he took his hand away and she moved to follow, her back arching, her ass lifting.

The action compelled him to do more. Explore what other things he could make her do with his touch.

Sitting up, he threw one leg over her and straddled her thighs. His cock rested in the crease of her ass and he rolled forward to press deeper between the plush globes. She was warm and soft and cushioned him perfectly.

Settled, he stroked his hands over her shoulders, her neck, down her spine. Massaging his fingers into her muscles, he delivered a sensual caress that had Sadie moaning and shifting under him.

Easing back, he dragged his fingers over the taut cheeks of her ass before digging in, pressing harder into the supple flesh of her delectable butt.

He wanted to kiss her there. Taste those luscious curves before moving on to the hot pussy tucked away beneath them.

"Alec?" Her voice was husky with sleep—laced with desire.

"Hmm..." He squeezed her ass, dug his thumbs into that shadowed crevice and pried it open.

Her pink folds glistened, her scent rising up to fill his nose, and he bent forward, took a deep breath. Except getting that close was a mistake.

There was no way he could stop himself from taking a taste of her.

She moaned and thrust her hips back toward him when he probed between her legs with his tongue.

It took no effort—and little encouragement on his part —to get Sadie to rise up onto her spread knees. He flipped onto his back and wiggled up the bed until that hot pussy was over his face.

Alex took his time. Lapping at her with gentle strokes. Used his teeth to skim the throbbing bundle of nerves popping from its protective hood. He held her ass cheeks in his palms, his fingers digging in to keep her in place while he savored every inch of her.

Her hips rocked. The flex and roll worked her flesh over his mouth, making it easy for him to sample all of her.

She moaned. Ground down. Moved faster.

"Alec." She panted above him. "I need..."

He smiled against her wet folds. "Don't worry. I've got you."

Licking and sucking, tugging lightly with his teeth, Alex ate her like a starving man at an all-you-can-eat buffet. He moved one hand from her ass and thrust two fingers deep into her sopping pussy. She spread her legs wider—rocked harder.

"That's it." He spoke into her slick flesh. "Take what you want. What you need."

Wrapping his lips around her clit he sucked hard and worked a third finger inside her.

A strangled cry split the air and Sadie slammed down on his face, grinding back and forth as she came apart, flooding his mouth and hand with wet heat.

Riding out her orgasm, Alex prayed he wouldn't embarrass himself and come all over his stomach. The last contractions gripped his fingers and he kept them buried deep as he moved out from under her.

He snagged a condom and quickly sheathed his

straining cock one handed. If he didn't get inside her this second, he'd go mad.

Alex wasn't sure how he managed it so fast but he had her ass pressed against his groin, her still-clenching pussy impaled on his cock before either of them took their next breath.

With a groan, he leaned over her and sank his teeth into the curve between neck and shoulder, pinning her in place, and pounded into her repeatedly.

His mind was blank of anything except the need to hit that spot, the one that was guaranteed to blow his head right off his shoulders. She squeezed him on the drive in and on the drag out.

Hot and hard, their bodies slammed together with wet slaps that matched the thumping in his chest, the one in his ears.

Blood rushed in a tidal surge of need that blurred his vision and stole his breath. Every part of him stretched tight—reached out with single-minded determination...

"Alec," Sadie cried out. Her pussy clamped down on his cock—squeezed him beyond pleasure.

It felt as if she were sucking his balls out through his cock. "*Fuck.*"

His breath caught. His hips stilled. Then he exploded.

Fractured into a million different razor-sharp pieces that sliced him to the bone.

He collapsed forward—pressed Sadie into the mattress with his full weight—and let the brutal euphoria take him.

Alex's heart beat against his ribs so hard he thought he

might be having a heart attack. Not to mention the fact his lungs didn't seem to be able to suck in air.

Sadie groaned and wiggled beneath him and it took all he had to roll off her.

Flopping to his back, he tried to find a sliver of sanity in the mish-mash of thoughts ricocheting around his head.

One thing kept coming around though. One thought above all others.

More.

No matter how their night together had started—and he hadn't put much thought into it beyond his desire to get her naked under him—he wasn't done.

As soon as he took a nap, regained his strength, he was getting himself more—much more—of Sadie Emerson.

CHAPTER 7

Sadie focused her blurry vision on the man sleeping soundly beside her.

Her college crush.

Alec Dane.

He was leaner than she remembered. Not that she'd ever seen him naked before.

She smiled.

A naked Alec was definitely a sight she could get used to.

Shame she didn't have her glasses so she could get a better look at him—examine him more closely—although, a fuzzy naked Alec wasn't anything to complain about.

He was half on his side, one leg bent up toward his chest, his arms wrapped around the pillow hugged to his chest. The broad expanse of his back was toward her and the sun streaming in through the window behind them bathed him in a golden glow.

She wanted to reach out and touch but when she did, her hand shook and she quickly pulled it back.

Touching him in the dark was completely different than doing it in the harsh light of day.

She took a deep breath and propped herself up on one elbow. If she couldn't bring herself to touch him, she'd continue to look.

His hair was short—the length no longer brushing his shoulders—the brown strands darker than she remembered them being in college.

The strong line of his jaw gave him a manly appeal. It had strengthened with age, turned him from boyishly good-looking to ruggedly handsome. No doubt about it, the boy she'd crushed on was all man now.

If he looked this good with her vision blurred, Sadie had to wonder if she'd be able to stand the sight of him with her glasses on.

He moved and the tattoo between his shoulder blades rippled, drawing her gaze.

She didn't remember him having it in college but something about it niggled at her mind.

She wanted to ask him when he'd gotten it—what it meant, had it hurt—except she couldn't bring herself to touch him while he slept, never mind wake him up and talk to him.

Just the thought of having to face him after all they'd done made her stomach cramp, her palms sweat, and her throat thicken.

Then again, that could be lust.

Even with her body still thrumming with satisfaction,

she couldn't deny she wanted more of the pleasure Alec could deliver. Stiff muscles and the minor aches she felt in places long ignored—and those never touched—brought back vivid memories.

Sadie couldn't decide if she was embarrassed or thrilled by their night together—by her daring actions.

Either way, she would definitely do it again. All of it.

Only this was supposed to be a one-night stand.

One night of fantasy with her college fantasy man.

And oh boy had it been one fantastic night.

Nothing her imagination conjured up compared to the real thing. It was quite possible Alec had ruined her for other men.

The things he'd done to her, the things she'd done to him, everything they'd done together. She couldn't imagine doing any of it with someone else.

Was that the one-night fantasy element or the man himself?

Back in college she'd heard rumors of his prowess. You had to be deaf, dumb, and dead not to hear the talk about any of the jocks who made their way through the female population on and off campus.

Not that Sadie had been one of those lucky women or in their social circle.

She remembered overhearing one particular conversation where a girl had regaled the staying power of a guy from the group Alec hung around with. Apparently the guy could go all night.

Sadie specifically remembered the girl giving graphic details about licking the intricate tattoo between...

Sadie sucked in a breath, her gaze flying to Alec's upper back.

Tattoo!

"Oh God," she whispered behind the shaky fingers of one hand as she wiggled backward on the bed.

She stared at Alec's back. The dark lines of the tattoo merging together to form a picture she couldn't make out without her glasses, but could now clearly picture in her mind.

Memories from college, of shirtless guys playing football in the green space between the dorms, of the sweat, the muscles, *the tattoo*.

Alec Dane didn't have a tattoo on his back.

Alexander Dean did.

"*Oh my God!*" She'd slept with the wrong guy.

CHAPTER 8

S ADIE STOOD on the sidewalk outside Alex's place and couldn't remember how she got there. The panic exploding inside her left her spinning—breathless—and she sucked in air faster than a vacuum cleaner.

She had to get to Mel's.

Tugging her phone from her skirt pocket, she fumbled it before clutching it tight in her sweaty hand and tapping at the screen, getting more and more frustrated when the stupid thing wouldn't do what she wanted.

A sob hitched in her throat. Squeezed her chest.

Hands shaking, Sadie squinted at the screen, took a deep breath, and tried to calm down. Finally she got the thing to work and brought it to her ear. It rang twice before Mel answered.

"Hey, how's—"

"I need you to come get me," Sadie blurted.

"Sure, no worries, but how was it? Everything you imagined? Was he as good as they say?" While Sadie sucked in air like a world champ, Mel didn't breathe at all.

"Mel!" Her chest heaved with a fractured breath. "Please." She gulped for air. "Just come get me."

"Sadie? What's wrong?" Mel's tone changed completely. Gone was the inquisitive best friend, replaced by the kill-for-you-and-bury-the-body best friend. "Did that asshole hurt you? I'll kill him."

"N-no. Please." She swallowed back a sob and prayed the flashing sparkles in her vision went away. "C-come get me."

"Where are you?" Sadie could hear keys rattling in the background.

"I..." *Oh God. Where am I?* Glancing around frantically, Sadie looked for anything she recognized. "I... I don't know," she cried.

"Okay. Calm down. Take a breath."

"I don't know..." Tears threatened. "Where I am."

"All right. All right. Keep calm. Here's what you're going to do. Stay on the phone with me and see if you can flag down a cab."

Sadie searched the street. Wherever she was, it wasn't out of the way. There was plenty of traffic, both vehicular and pedestrian. She ignored the looks from those close enough to witness her meltdown and, spotting what she thought was a cab heading toward her, she stepped to the curb and waved her arm in the air. "I think I see one."

"Flag it down."

"I am." The car swerved toward the curb and pulled up

with a screech of brakes.

Sadie quickly opened the rear door and slid inside. She moved the phone away from her mouth and gave the driver Mel's address.

Leaning back against the seat, she closed her eyes and focused back on Mel. "I'm in a cab."

"Okay. I'll wait out front."

Sadie took her first deep breath since realizing she'd slept with Alex Dean instead of Alec Dane. "Thanks. I don't have much cash on me, if the fare's more than—"

"Don't worry about that. I've got you covered."

And that was why, in spite of their differences, she and Mel were best friends.

Whenever Sadie fucked-up socially—and she did a lot —Mel was there to help.

She sniffled. "T-thank you."

Mel sighed. "Sadie. Hold it together until you get here." Her best friend knew her so well. "I'm staying right here, you don't have to talk. Just focus on breathing. In and out. Nice and slow. C'mon, do it with me."

Proving her BBF worth for the millionth time in the years since they'd met, Mel breathed into the phone in a steady deep rhythm.

Sucking in a gulp of air, Sadie took Mel's advice and concentrated on matching Mel's inhales and exhales, focusing on taking one deep breath after another and somehow managed to keep it together.

Until the cabdriver had been paid and Mel had pushed her through the front door and slammed it behind them.

Then Sadie let go. And cried until her eyes were red

and her throat was raw and she passed out exhausted on Mel's bed.

42

CHAPTER 9

Alex didn't need to open his eyes to know the bed beside him was empty.

He opened them anyway.

The pillow beside his had a dent where Sadie's head had been. But when he slid his hand across the sheet, none of her warmth remained.

Getting out of bed held no appeal. He'd planned to explain the mix up, convince her it didn't matter, and spend the day with her. Find out everything she'd done since the last time he'd seen her. Get to know her in a way he never had in college.

Now the day stretched out in front of him. Bleak and empty.

Seeing her at the club had been an unexpected surprise —a good one—and Alex had spent ages watching her sleep in the predawn light while coming up with ways to persuade her that one night—no matter how it had come about—was just the beginning.

Alex couldn't explain the emotions rolling through him. He'd barely known her in college. Sure he'd whipped up some amazing fantasies around her and the spark of attraction he'd felt; she'd been a star in his spank-bank for most of his final year in school, but this...

This was so far out of his comfort zone.

He'd never wanted anyone the way he did Sadie. He wasn't sure what made her different. She certainly wasn't the first woman he'd lusted after. But she was the first to make him want to know everything about her. The first he could imagine building a life with.

Not even his one long term girlfriend had inspired such thoughts.

Maybe she left a note...

He threw his legs over the side of the bed and jumped to his feet. Scanning the room, he check the tops of both bedside tables, the dresser, the bed, under it, he even looked through the pile of clothes he'd discarded in his haste to get them both naked.

Nothing.

If it wasn't for the indented pillow and the scent of her still lingering in the room—on his skin—Alex would think he'd dreamed the whole thing. Think the vivid memories replaying in his head were nothing more than new fantasies his libido had conjured up.

Scrubbing a hand down his face, he walked to the bathroom. He took care of business then decided coffee would do more to clear his head than a shower at this point. Plus, he didn't want to wash away Sadie's scent.

He wasn't ready to let go of their night. Not yet. Hell, he wasn't sure he ever would be.

Tugging on a pair of clean jeans, he zipped but left the button undone and made his way to the kitchen.

"Wow. For a guy who got lucky last night you sure don't look happy."

Alex's gaze swung to the breakfast counter where his friend and host, John, sat. He shrugged and continued toward the coffee machine.

"Guess the morning after didn't go so well," John said behind him.

"Hard to go well when it doesn't happen," Alex grumbled.

"Ah, so she *was* sneaking out. Not that she was doing it all that sneakily. What with the mumbling under her breath and bumping into furniture, the wall."

Alex turned to face John. "What?"

John tipped his head in the direction of the front door. "She hightailed it out of here thirty minutes ago. Bumping into shit and mumbling about making a mistake."

Alex scowled and took a step forward. "You saw Sadie leave and didn't stop her?"

His friend held up his hands. "Whoa. I didn't know I was supposed to barricade the door."

"Sorry." Alex gripped the back of his neck and squeezed. "I—"

"Wait." John sat up straight. "Sadie? Sadie-Emerson-hot-sexy-math-tutor Sadie?"

Alex nodded.

John's head swung toward the door. "Oh my God. *That* was Stammering Sadie?"

"Hey." Alex took another step forward. "Cut that shit out."

John eyed him.

"She doesn't have a stutter."

Okay, she had stuttered a bit back in college, and she had a couple of times last night, except all the times he'd overheard Sadie talking when she didn't know he was there, she'd not once stumbled over her words. It seemed the guys on the football team had made her nervous.

Understandable, when they were all so much bigger than her physically, and most of them had expected every woman to fall at their feet. Some of the shit they used to say to her...

God, if he could go back he'd stop the sexual innuendo.

John held up his hands again. "Okay, man. Whatever you say."

Alex's frown deepened.

Shaking his head, John said, "You know, I have to hand it to you, she's smokin' hot without those old lady glasses."

Alex growled.

John grinned.

Turning his back, he set about making a coffee. He knew his friend was trying to get a rise out him. John had been one of the biggest stirrers in their group.

"So...I'm guessing you didn't get her number."

He glanced over his shoulder and glared at his friend.

"What would it be worth if I could get it for you?"

John's smug smile only irritated him more, but if he could get Sadie's number...

Leaning back against the counter, Alex watched his possibly soon-to-be ex-friend over the top of his mug. Taking a sip, he let the silence lengthen—thicken.

John's smile drooped, along with his shoulders. "Fine. I'll get it for you."

Alex grinned. John never could hold out on him. He was one of the few friends from college he still spoke to on a regular basis.

"But you'll owe me." John stood. "Let me get my phone."

Alex waited for John to come back from his room and contemplated what to do.

Sadie had snuck out without so much as a goodbye, never mind a *I had a great time, here's my number give me a call so we can do it again*, so did that mean she didn't want to see him? Did she regret having sex with him? And what about when he told her who he really was?

She'd had a good time—they both had—he'd made sure of that. Although his gut told him mind-blowing sex between them didn't require effort.

"Here." John handed Alex his phone.

He looked down at the contact John had pulled up. "Who's Melinda Shaw? I thought you said you could get me Sadie's number?" Alex stared at his friend. The name was familiar but it wasn't the woman he was after.

"Melinda, aka Mel, is Sadie's best friend. You have to convince *her* to give you Sadie's info."

"Mel." Alex groaned.

"What?"

"Sadie said she was staying with Mel until she leaves."

"Leaves? Where's she going?"

Alex ran a hand through his hair. "I don't know. We didn't get to that before..." He swallowed, memories of pushing Sadie up against the wall of the elevator flashing through his mind.

John laughed. "Well, Mel will know."

"But will she tell me?"

CHAPTER 10

ALEX STARED at the new contact on his phone.

He'd left John in the kitchen and retreated to the bedroom. He wasn't sure what he would say or if Mel would even answer an unknown number.

Taking a deep breath he hit call and brought the device to his ear.

It rang and rang and when voicemail cut in he still didn't know what to say so he hung up.

With a smack to his forehead, he muttered, "Fuck, I'm an idiot."

Leaving a message would have been better than hanging up. Now he'd just look like a dick when he called back.

Too bad. He wanted Sadie's contact details and Mel was the door he had to go through to get them.

He had to call back. Now or later wouldn't make a difference to how his call would be received. Best to get it done. That way if it went to voicemail again and he had to leave a message he could follow it up with a text or two later.

Not surprised when his second call also went to voicemail, Alex was ready. "Hi Melinda, this is Alex Dean. I'm looking to get in contact with Sadie Emerson. If you could give her this number to call me back that would be great. Thanks."

As he ended the call he realized he should have asked if Sadie had made it home okay. Deciding the best course of action for that was a text, he brought up the app and quickly typed out a message.

Alex: Hi, Alex again. Just want to check Sadie got home safely.

Shocked to see the little bubble that meant Mel was replying pop up, he waited, breath held, to see what she'd say.

Melinda: She made it.

He waited for more.

When five minutes passed and there weren't any more words, he had to accept what little he had for now. Pushing it by calling again, or even messaging wouldn't be in his best interests. He couldn't leave it at that though. He'd wait an hour or so and reach out again.

He'd shower and head out for some breakfast. Maybe see if John wanted to tag along. They hadn't really caught up much in spite of Alex bunking in his friend's spare room.

A plan in place, he stripped out of his jeans and went into the bathroom.

John's place was small but well appointed. Both bedrooms had their own en suite and were the size of a master. Perfect for a bachelor who had the occasional guest.

The layout was similar to a remodel he had designed in New York City just before he'd gone out on his own and started his company.

That job had been one of the reasons Alex had decided he'd had enough of working for a large architectural firm. None of the easily fitted environmentally friendly furnishings and fixtures he'd suggested had been taken into account and he'd finally moved in the direction he'd always wanted to go.

And he was doing it holding the reins.

In two years he'd made a name for himself. People all over the country sought him out, waited for him to be available for a consult. He tried to stick close to home but it wasn't unusual for him to have a job in a different state or on the other side of the country.

One thing about being his own boss meant he could take a few days off when he wanted. He'd surrounded himself with skilled, dedicated employees, ones who shared his vision of designing and constructing functional, comfortable, practical, and environmentally responsible buildings.

Flicking on the water, Alex stepped under the shower. He sucked in a breath as the icy blast hit him head on and slid down to his toes. Ignoring the shudder that racked him, he grabbed the soap and began to wash his body. He tried not to think about the symbolism of washing Sadie away.

He definitely wouldn't think about it.

No. He'd keep positive thoughts and do everything he could to ensure he hadn't seen the last of her. That option wasn't acceptable. He couldn't imagine not being with her again, not after last night. The connection they shared was special and he knew she'd felt it too.

No, not seeing her again was definitely not an option. Whatever it took, he'd find a way.

He made quick work of cleaning up, and to be honest, he didn't care if he didn't do a thorough job; if a little of Sadie's scent remained he'd be happy.

Turning the water off he stepped out, picked up a towel, briskly scrubbed it over his body, then wrapped it around his hips. Walking back into the bedroom he considered what to do for the rest of the day other than attempt to talk to Sadie.

The guys were all getting together and going out again tonight but Alex didn't really want to go. He'd had his fill of clubbing last night.

He had one leg in his jeans when his phone buzzed. Diving for it, his leg got caught up in his pants and he tripped, doing a header straight into the side of the bed.

Crumpled on the floor, he stared up at the ceiling and worked out two things.

One, he was pretty sure he'd just twisted his bad knee.

Two, he was way more invested in Sadie than he'd thought.

If that message wasn't from her or Mel he didn't want to see it.

There was no denying the anticipation thrumming through his veins. Or the fact his cock had thickened with only the thought of Sadie being on the other end of that message.

He needed to calm down. If he rushed at this, he could fuck it up. The last thing he wanted to do was scare Sadie off. Curling up, he reached across the bed and dragged his phone closer.

The screen lit up revealing the message, and Alex couldn't help the bark of laughter that burst out of him.

Alec: Hey, sorry to miss you this weekend. Catch you next time.

How ironic that the person messaging him was the person responsible for his night with Sadie.

CHAPTER 11

Sadie entered Mel's kitchen and found her friend on the phone.

Mel's eyes popped wide and she sucked in a breath, blurted, "I gotta go. I'll call you back," into the phone, hung up, and shoved it into her back pocket.

Eyeing her friend suspiciously, she asked, "Who was that?"

"Ah, um, work."

"Work?" Sadie didn't believe her. Mel couldn't lie to save her life but it was obviously something she didn't want to share. "Anything important? You don't have to babysit me. If you need to go, go."

Mel forced a smile. "Nope. All good." She turned, avoiding Sadie's gaze and pulled a tray out of the oven. "So, now that you've finished freaking out...tell me all about it."

"I slept with the wrong Alec."

Mel glanced over her shoulder, her eyebrows rising to

her hairline. "The wrong Alec? What the hell does that mean?"

Sadie pulled out a chair at the cute little two-seater table Mel had attached to the wall in her kitchen and with a sigh, dropped into the seat, lowered her forehead to the hard timber and banged it twice.

"Hey!" Mel shoved an oven mitt under Sadie's forehead. "You'll hurt yourself."

The scent of warm chocolate surrounded her. "Has to feel better than humiliation."

Mel gave her hair a gentle tug. "Sit up and talk to me."

Sadie lifted her head and a mug appeared in front of her. The aroma of hazelnut-laced coffee floated around her, mingling with the chocolate and making Sadie's mouth water.

"Drink." A plate slid across the table. "Eat."

She glanced up at Mel and arched one eyebrow. "Your famous chocolate brownies?"

"Hell yes." Mel plopped into the chair opposite with her own plate of heaven. "Double-choc brownies are a cure-all medicine."

Sadie's other eyebrow rose. "Is that your expert medical opinion?"

Mel smirked and shoved a whole brownie square in her mouth, her eyelids fluttering low. "Mmmm…"

Sadie picked up the smallest square from her own plate and nibbled the corner.

Mel laughed. "For God's sake. Just eat the damn thing."

"I'm not really hungry…"

"You don't need hunger to eat my chocolate brownies."

Mel picked up her mug. "So explain this 'wrong Alec' thing to me."

"I didn't sleep with Alec Dane. I slept with *Alex Dean*."

Mel shrugged. "Does it matter?"

Sadie's mouth dropped open. Snapped shut. "Does it... Of course it matters!"

"Why?"

"Because I thought I was going home with Alec Dane!"

Mel was shaking her head. "Was he good?"

"W-what?" Heat flashed through her, scorched her cheeks, and swelled between her thighs.

"I'll take that blush on your face as a yes."

"Good or bad makes no difference. I didn't sleep with the guy I thought I was sleeping with."

"Well, personally, I'm hoping you didn't sleep at all." Mel popped another whole brownie square in her mouth.

"Mel!"

Mel arched an eyebrow and chewed her mouthful while Sadie squirmed in her seat. She hated it when Mel looked at her like that. It usually meant she'd be on the receiving end of a best-friend lecture about her lack of social etiquette.

Unfortunately, Mel always seemed to have valid points and arguments that left Sadie wondering why she hadn't just done what Mel suggested to begin with.

Sadie sighed and leaned back in her chair. Best to give in sooner than later. "Don't keep me in suspense. Lecture away."

"I'm not going to lecture you but I *am* going to point out a few things. Last night was about letting loose. About doing something you've always wanted to do. About being daring."

"Trust me to turn it into a daring mistake," she muttered then stuffed her mouth full of chocolatey goodness.

"Did you get off?"

Another wave of heat flooded her. Sadie tightened her thighs in an attempt to ease the ache throbbing in her sex.

"Thought so." Mel nodded. "The night wasn't a mistake. You went home with a hot guy and he delivered."

"And then some," Sadie mumbled around the brownie.

"What was that?" Mel leaned closer.

She swallowed her mouthful and took a sip of her coffee. Memories of last night played through her mind and a rush of air left Sadie's lungs as more heat washed over her.

"I'm going to assume by your behavior that I've made my point."

"What point?" Whatever Mel was getting at had gone right over her head. Or she was too busy flipping through the movie reel of memories of her night with Alex to get it.

"The point is, it doesn't really matter what the guy's name is or isn't, or who he is or isn't. The whole point was for you to have a fantastic night. With *who* was always irrelevant."

"It was never like that with Patrick," Sadie admitted.

"Hmph." Mel waved her hand. "There's no comparison. Patrick couldn't find your clit if you gave him a detailed map, exact coordinates, and fucking GPS," Mel argued.

"That's a little harsh."

"So you're saying Patrick got you off?" Mel laughed. "Sorry." She covered her mouth with one hand but she couldn't hide her grin.

"He tried."

"Oh God." Mel pushed back her chair and doubled over laughing.

Sadie crossed her arms and glared at her best friend. "Not all guys are as experienced with women as Alex."

Mel sat up straight. "You know, I don't actually recall either Alex or Alec going through women all that much. In fact, Alex Dean had a steady girlfriend most of the way through college if memory serves, and I'm pretty sure Alec Dane was the same."

"What's that got to do with anything?"

Mel shrugged. "Nothing I guess."

Sadie shook her head and stood. "I'm going to grab a shower. Do you want to go out for pizza when I'm done?" Not that she was hungry, not with one of Mel's brownies filling her belly. Regardless of her full or not state, hanging around the house would just lead to her brooding over last night, and she needed to wipe the memories from her mind and move on.

"Sure. We'll go to Emilio's."

"What time do you want to go?"

Mel glanced at the wall clock. "In about an hour?"

"Sounds good." Sadie picked up the last brownie on her plate and grinned at her friend. An hour was a long time and who could resist a double-choc brownie? "This will keep me going."

Mel sighed as she picked up another brownie. "Unlike

some, this is the closest I've gotten to a man-made orgasm in months."

Sadie's pulse kicked up a gear. Until last night, she would have said Mel's brownies were better than an orgasm.

Oh, how wrong she'd been.

CHAPTER 12

ALEX PUSHED OPEN the door to Emilio's with his stomach in a knot. He'd been sitting down the street waiting for Mel's text for the last fifteen minutes. His phone had finally buzzed and he practically ran to get here.

He couldn't remember ever being this nervous in the past. Or this eager. But then everything about Sadie was different from any other woman. He'd never felt an instant connection or one this deep, not even with Meghan, his college girlfriend.

Scanning the tables, he spotted his target in the far corner. Sadie's back was to him and he wondered if Mel had done that so she wouldn't see him coming. Sadie had run from him once already and he had to appreciate Mel's help, even if it had been unintentional.

The closer he got to their table, the more apprehensive he felt about the plan he and Mel had devised. He was sweating and his heart rate was elevated.

60

There was no denying it—there was definitely some-thing unique about Sadie.

"Hey, Sadie." Alex stopped beside her chair. "Sorry I missed you this morning. You really wore me out." He grinned as he pulled out the chair beside her and sat.

"Alex!" Her voice squeaked and her hazel eyes looked huge behind the sexy red-framed glasses she wore. "W-what are you doing h-here?"

He chuckled. "Same as you, I'd think."

"I...um..."

"Have you ordered? I haven't eaten here in ages. Anything you'd recommend?" Alex figured if he kept talk-ing, she couldn't tell him to take a hike.

"Pizza or pasta?" Mel asked. "You can't go wrong with either here. And we haven't ordered yet. Why don't you join us?"

"Mel!"

Alex smiled at Sadie's obvious discomfort. At least she wasn't indifferent to him. He'd take affecting her any way he could right now. "I'd love to. What were you two thinking of having?"

"Sadie wanted a pizza so we were going to split a large, but now that you're here, you two can split and I'll get pasta." Mel smiled a closed lipped smile.

To Alex's eyes it seemed a little forced, and when he looked at Sadie, he found her glaring at her friend with narrowed eyes.

"Sure. I eat anything but anchovies." He glanced around for a server so they could order before Sadie objected. Or bolted.

"Wow. You and Sadie have the same tastes. She hates anchovies too." Mel stared at him, her gaze tinged with desperation.

Alex smiled in the hope of reassuring her—of what, he wasn't sure, but he did his best to paste on a warm, confident grin. Unfortunately he didn't have a clue what to say now.

A waitress arrived at their table saving him from the uncomfortable silence that threatened to settle over them.

"Okay, ladies, what are we having?" he asked, and leaned toward Sadie to read the menu on the table in front of her.

Sadie moved away, but not before Alex got a good lungful of her scent. His body tightened, his groin throbbing as blood filled his cock.

Damn. He wanted her again. It was as though he hadn't spent all night buried inside her.

"I, um...pick whatever." Sadie pushed her chair back. "I need to use the bathroom."

She was gone before Alex blinked. He glanced at Mel with one eyebrow raised.

Mel shrugged as she grabbed the strap of her bag off the back of her chair. "You get to her. But she's just given me the perfect opportunity to escape."

"What?" he asked as Mel got to her feet.

"Tell her I got called in to work."

"You're leaving?" Did his voice just go up a couple of octaves?

She grinned at him and patted his cheek. "Don't look so worried. I'm betting on you to win Sadie over."

"Win her over?"

Mel laughed. "Man, the look on your face is priceless." She gripped his shoulder, her fingers digging in. "Just so we're clear. Hurt her and I'll hunt you down."

He swallowed. "I..." It didn't matter that he had no clue what to say. Mel was gone.

"Ahem."

Alex turned to the waitress standing beside him. "What can I get you?" she asked with a bored look and a pen poised over her order pad.

"Um, a large pizza with everything, but no anchovies. Oh, and I'll have a beer, whatever you've got—and a refill on that." He pointed to Sadie's half-empty glass.

"No worries. The pizza will take about ten minutes and I'll be right back with the drinks in a minute." She picked up the menus and hurried away.

Alex nodded, forcing a smile even though she was already gone. As he watched the waitress walk away, he spotted Sadie coming back from the bathroom. She moved toward him, her long legs bringing her closer with each breath.

The sight had him thinking of last night and having those sexy limbs wrapped around him, straddling him— spread wide for him.

Sweat popped out on his forehead, his upper lip, and a bead rolled down the middle of his back.

Holy hell.

Sadie Emerson had him by the balls, and not only did he think she didn't have a clue, but Alex feared if she did know she wouldn't care.

CHAPTER 13

SADIE LEFT the bathroom still unsure how to deal with seeing Alex again. Weaving her way through the tables she tried to decide what she wanted to do other than jump the man. That wasn't an option.

Reaching the table, she slid back into her seat and scowled at the vacant chair opposite her. "Mel skipped out, didn't she?"

Alex nodded beside her.

"What excuse did she tell you to give me?" God, she was going to kill her best friend.

"Does it matter?"

She sighed. "I guess not."

"I ordered us a pizza with the lot. No anchovies."

"Sounds fine."

"Sadie—"

"I'm sorr—"

Their gazes connected as they spoke over each other.

Alex smiled and Sadie's stomach dipped. She remembered kissing that mouth. Remember that mouth kissing her.

All over.

A shudder rolled through her. "I, um...about this morning."

His hand cupped hers on the table. "It's fine."

"No. It's not." She straightened her spine. Pulled her hand from beneath his. "I don't normally do that. Actually I've never done that."

Alex grinned. "Me either."

"What?" Sadie stared at him. Did he expect her to believe that?

"I'm not in the habit of picking women up in clubs and taking them home." He shrugged. "But then you're not just any woman."

"What does that mean?" She could see the genuine honesty in Alex's eyes.

"I had a thing for you in college."

Sadie jerked back in her seat. "What?"

He reached for her hand again, weaving his fingers through hers before she could pull away. "I used to sit in those tutoring sessions and think about taking more than your glasses off."

She laughed. "Sure. Right. You and every other guy on the team."

"You'd be surprised."

Sadie couldn't believe the bullshit flowing out of Alex's mouth. If he wanted to have sex with her again, he was going about it the wrong way. She tugged her hand from his.

"Look, Alex, you already got me into bed, so sweet talk isn't necessary and I have to be honest. I wasn't wearing my glasses or contact lenses last night and I thought you were someone else." There. That ought to cut this farce short.

"I know."

"Huh?" He knew she'd mistaken him for someone else?

"You called me Alec Dane at the club. I didn't correct you. I knew you thought you were going home with Alec and I let you keep thinking that because I wanted you. Bad."

"I—" He pressed two fingers to her lips.

"No. Don't say anything. Let's just eat dinner. Catch up on what we've both been doing since school."

Sadie blinked. Was he serious? There was no way she could sit here and pretend to be old friends catching up. Not when her memory bank kept throwing up vivid images of their night together on her mind's eye.

"Please, Sadie. Just dinner."

She couldn't ignore the pleading edge to his words. Or the thrill it gave her knowing he wanted to spend time with her in spite of the way they'd connected and the way she'd left.

The waitress arrived with drinks. "Here you go. Your pizza won't be much longer."

Sadie kept her gaze locked with Alex's the whole time. His fingers still pressed against her lips and she couldn't stop herself from flicking out her tongue—tasting his skin.

His eyes dilated, his nostrils flaring as he sucked in a harsh breath and pulled his hand away. "*Sadie.*"

Her name was a raspy growl and a shiver stole through her. "Okay. Just dinner."

Alex took a deep breath, then grinned. "Great. So tell me, what have you done since I left college?"

Sadie smiled. It wasn't as if they'd ever really spoken back in college. Not unless it was about math. "Um, not much. Graduated. A year early. Worked at a finance firm here in Miami until a week ago."

"Finance." Alex smiled as he picked up his beer and took a swig. "Why am I not surprised by that?"

She shrugged. "I like numbers. And those with dollar signs in front of them especially."

"So what now?"

"What?"

"You said you're not at that job anymore."

"Oh, right. I accepted a job with the Economic Development Board of Winter Lake—it's a small mountain town in New York. I'm moving up there next week." She swallowed. "Which is why we shouldn't do this."

"Do what?" he asked, his gaze on the beer in his hand.

Sadie gestured between them with her hand. "This. Whatever this is."

"Dinner?" he questioned with a cheeky grin on his lips, his eyes now back on hers.

"I'm leaving in two days. Nothing can come of us spending any more time together."

"So you're putting last night firmly in the one-night stand box?"

God, she didn't want to. Alex looked a thousand times better with her glasses on. But she was leaving. And he was here. Sadie shook her head. "I'm moving hundreds of miles away."

Alex smiled. A smile that had Sadie's nerves twitching. "Let's not worry about that now. We'll talk and enjoy tonight. Let tomorrow look after itself."

Sadie wanted to. Except she knew if she looked deep enough she'd find a kernel of hope that being with Alex wouldn't be finished along with the last bite of pizza.

CHAPTER 14

ALEX BLEW out a breath and sat back in his chair. He swallowed the last bite of pizza and tried to remember enjoying a meal with any other woman more than he'd enjoyed the last hour with Sadie. To his mind it indicated his decision to pursue her was the right move.

She'd lost her slight stammer after the first few minutes and he had to take it as a sign she was no longer nervous around him. He was certainly comfortable being with her. Well, if he didn't take into account the hard-on being crushed by his jeans. She'd had him in a constant state of arousal since he'd seen her across the club the night before.

Where this was going was anyone's guess, but he hoped it was far. The fact she wanted to put a stop to anything further between them because of her move didn't faze him.

He'd neglected to tell her he didn't actually live in Miami. He hadn't since he'd graduated from college and taken a job with a Brooklyn-based architectural firm

He was out on his own now and living in his hometown, doing local work as well as all over the country.

It had taken everything he had not to react when she'd mentioned his hometown. He wasn't sure when or if he planned to share his usual place of residence.

The idea of surprising her once she moved to Winter Lake was very appealing. Alex could almost picture the look on her face when they *bumped* into each other. Probably the day she arrived. It was a small town after all.

"You didn't tell me where in Winter Lake you're staying?" He picked up his beer and finished it off.

"Oh. Well, luckily for me, my boss has a friend who was looking for someone to help cut the cost of his place so I'm leasing the top-floor loft."

"Whereabouts?"

"One street back from Lake Front. Can you believe that's the name of the main street? I know Miami is a 'beach' town but I'm really looking forward to living close to the water. I can't wait to check it all out."

Alex choked. Fuck. She was going to live one street over from his current place. He was living in one of his rentals while his place across the lake in the small town of Broken Bay was being renovated.

"You okay?" Sadie leaned over and patted his back awkwardly.

"Yep. All good," he gasped. "Went down the wrong way." Alex tried for a reassuring smile but didn't think he pulled it off with the way she was looking at him. He waved her away. "I'm good. Honest."

She inched back in her seat.

With a grin, Alex reached for his wallet. "Let's get out of here." He pushed back his chair and tossed some bills on the table. More than enough to cover their meal and tip.

"Oh." Sadie frowned.

"What?" Alex didn't like the troubled look in her eyes.

"Mel's gone."

"Ah…" He hoped she'd elaborate further because he was clueless as to what Mel's absence meant.

"She's my ride," Sadie explained as she stood.

"No problem. I can give you a lift." He'd borrowed John's car. He hadn't bothered hiring one when he flew in two days ago, not when his friend worked from home and offered his rarely used car for Alex's use.

"No, that's okay. I can get a cab." She slipped the strap of her bag over one shoulder. "I don't want to put you out."

"It's no trouble." He placed his hand on her lower back and urged her from the restaurant. "Plus my mother would kill me if she knew I let my date find her own way home."

Sadie's head swung around and her wide eyes bore into his. "This wasn't a date. We're not dating. We can't date. I'm leaving."

Whoa. Way to get her point across. Alex hid his smile. "She'd still kill me, and you don't want that on your conscience."

She frowned. Her brow at the top of her nose looked so cute all crinkled that he couldn't help himself. He leaned over and kissed her forehead.

Sucking in a breath, she jerked away but Alex didn't let her reaction worry him.

Before Sadie could say anything, he steered her out

onto the sidewalk and grabbed her hand. "The car is this way." He tempered the urge to run—now that he had her hand in his—and kept his pace easy.

They were quiet as they walked down the street. People were out and about enjoying the early evening and Alex had to admit he loved the feeling of Sadie beside him. He wondered if he'd get to take a walk along the lake with her when she moved to his hometown. Or perhaps he could take her to see all the sights the mountain region had to offer. He'd bet money she'd love the view from Lake View Lookout.

"Have you ever been to New York state?"

"No. I interviewed through an agency then over a video chat with the board chairman and the mayor."

"Are you looking forward to it? The move?" Alex slowed his pace. The longer they took to get to the car, the more time he could spend with Sadie.

"Yes. I'm excited about the new job and of course, having my own space will be great. I shared an apartment before so I'm definitely happy to be able to do what I want, when I want from now on."

"Now you can dance naked in the kitchen." He grinned at her.

Sadie laughed. "I don't think I'll go quite that far. Just having the option is enough freedom for me."

John's SUV came into view and Alex slowed his steps further. "When do you leave?"

"Monday morning. I'll have a full week to get settled in my new place before I start my job." She was smiling.

"You look really happy at the prospect." In Alex's opinion, she glowed with her excitement. He wished she'd have that reaction to him. Although he wasn't giving up hope that she might eventually.

"I am. It's what I've wanted for as long as I can remember." She swung their joined hands between them.

"What, no white picket fences, kids, and happy-ever-after dreams?" He wasn't sure why he brought up the topic, except that he could picture her there. Him beside her.

Alex swallowed over the lump in his throat. He'd never had a clear view of the future before. Other than his goal to be one of the top architects in the country, hell the world, he'd had no real life goals.

Sadie shrugged, the motion jiggling their hands. "I was never one of those girls."

He arched an eyebrow. "Oh?"

"You know, the kind who plays house with her Barbies or baby dolls. I was into counting money and reading. And if you listen to my mother, I was more interested in pulling stuff apart and putting it together than playing with it. Not your typical girl, according to her."

"And some guy hasn't made you think of home and family?" Why was he pursuing this line of conversation? If he wouldn't look like an idiot he'd slap himself upside the head.

"Nope." They'd stopped walking and she looked up at him. "What about you? Any girl made you think about happy-ever-afters?"

Alex grinned. "The jury's still out on that. I'll let you know when it's in." He used his grip on her hand to tug her closer, leaned forward, and brought his mouth an inch from hers. "I'm gonna kiss you now, Sadie."

He didn't give her time to protest before slanting his mouth over hers. She tasted sweet and spicy—soda and pizza. Alex took his time. Trailed his tongue along the seam of her lips in a gentle stroke that had her melting into him.

Wrapping his arms around her waist, he drew her in until they were pressed together from chest to thigh. He wanted more but this wasn't the place. Still, he thrust his tongue into her mouth and kissed her with all the burning passion she inspired in him.

She moaned, her body going soft in his hold, as though her bones and muscles were liquifying beneath the heat of their blazing need.

He nipped at her bottom lip. "Come home with me."

Her eyelids fluttered open, her breath caressing his face in fast puffs. "I..."

"Please." Alex rocked his cock against her. "Give me one more night to get my fill of you."

CHAPTER 15

Sadie's back hit the wall of the elevator as Alex's tongue slid into her mouth.

God, he could kiss.

Her bag slipped from her shoulder as they came to a stop and the doors opened. Alex pulled away and stared down at her for long seconds. Long enough for the doors to close.

Hitting the button to open the doors again, he said, "C'mon," and grabbed her hand in a hold identical to last night.

Sadie's tummy dropped. She didn't want this to be their last night. He'd gotten under her skin and she had no doubt she'd see him again if she wasn't booked on a one-way flight out of town Monday morning.

Shaking the depressing thoughts from her head, she re-shouldered her bag and followed Alex down the hall, where he opened the door to his friend's apartment.

Like last night, she'd take tonight for what it was. She'd take as much of him as she could get and treasure all the memories when she was gone.

Alex led her into the apartment without turning on any lights. He dragged her through the bedroom door, spun her around, and pushed her against the wall. Shutting the door, he switched on the light. "I wanna go slow. Take my time and savor, but Sadie…"

He kissed her. Hard and deep with lots of tongue. It was more eat-her-alive than a kiss.

"I can't." His voice shook. His fingers dug in where they held her hips pressed against his. "Tell me I can take whatever I want."

"W-whatever you want." She had no choice. She couldn't say no to Alex. Didn't want to. Last night might have been a daring mistake but tonight wasn't.

Tonight she was taking Mel's advice and going after what she wanted.

And she wanted Alex Dean.

She wanted him with a need so sharp it would leave scars.

She dropped her bag and yanked at his shirt. Pushed it up over his washboard abs to his chest and growled with frustration when she couldn't shove it higher.

Alex laughed and, reaching one hand over his head, grabbed the back of his shirt. In a move so smooth he had to have done it a million times, he whipped his top off and dropped it on the floor at their feet.

"Now you."

She didn't need to be told twice. With trembling

fingers, she unbuttoned her blouse and let it slip from her shoulders. Alex flicked the front clasp of her bra open as she undid her slacks. Kicking off her flip-flops, she pushed her pants down her legs as he did the same with his own.

The sound of their harsh breathing was the only noise in the room. Her gaze traveled the length of him. From head to toes, Sadie looked her fill.

Damn, the man was built.

"Gorgeous."

Nodding, she murmured, "Yes. Yes, you are."

Alex laughed as he picked her up and walked to the bed. "I was talking about you."

"Oh." Heat flooded her face.

He grinned before he took them down to the bed. She landed on top of him, their naked bodies pressed together in all the right places. "Let's start with you on top."

A shiver ran through her. "O-okay." She remembered last time. The thrill of being in control until he'd taken over and driven them both over the edge.

"Condom." He reached for the drawer beside the bed.

"I'll do it." She wanted to drive him crazy like last time. Wanted to feel the rush of power that having his cock in her hands gave her.

"I don't know if I can last if you do." He tore the packet open and held it out. "Make it quick."

She grinned. His jaw was hard, his eyes dilated until the brown was just an outline edging his black pupils. Taking the condom, Sadie sat up and moved back until his cock stood between them.

Sitting this close, it almost looked as though she were

the one with the erection. Giggling, she smoothed the protection down his length.

"What's so funny?" he asked. "A guy could get a complex with a sexy woman laughing at his dick."

Smiling she said, "From this angle it kinda looks like your cock is mine."

"It is yours." Alex gripped her hips and pulled her forward. "Yours to ride."

Holding on to his arm with one hand, Sadie used the other to grab his shaft and guide him in as she slowly sank down.

Her memories lied.

It felt a thousand times better than she remembered.

No wonder she couldn't say no when he'd asked her to come home with him again. If this was all she'd have—two nights of bliss—she was taking every second she could.

"Oh God," she moaned when her clit hit Alex's pubic bone.

He stretched her in ways she'd never imagined, and muscles tender from last night's marathon sex session twitched with pain and pleasure. She finally understood the meaning of *hurt so good*.

Glancing down, she took in the sight of Alex with clear vision. She rose up. Sank down. Heat and pressure spiraled through her. Picking up speed, she rode him.

Up, down. Squeeze, release.

"Fuck." Alex groaned. "You're killing me."

Sadie grinned and went a little faster, squeezed a little tighter. "But in a good way right?" she panted.

"Oh yeah." His hands moved from her hips to her

breasts; cupping them in his palms, he strummed her nipples with his thumbs. "The best way."

She shuddered, her head dropping forward, her glasses sliding down her nose. "Dammit." Turning her head, she used her shoulder to push them back.

"Do you want them off?" Alex asked.

Her rhythm faltered. "What?"

"Glasses." He let go of one breast to reach for them. "Do you want me to take them off?"

"No!"

"Ookay."

"I want to see you this time." She'd missed out on so much last night. She cursed herself for not wearing her new contacts tonight, but even with the possibility of her glasses falling off her face, she wasn't about to give up her clear view of Alex.

Not when after tonight, she'd never see him again.

CHAPTER 16

ALEX COULDN'T GET ENOUGH of the woman sprawled on top of him. If he'd had any doubt, she'd just obliterated it with the way she rode them both to orgasm.

Christ, he still hadn't caught his breath and it had been a good five minutes since they'd climaxed together.

"I'll move in a second," Sadie murmured.

"You're fine." The thought of letting her go had his arms tightening around her.

"Mmm..."

Alex listened as Sadie's breathing evened out and her body went lax. He had to work out how to keep this woman in his life. She'd blindsided him with more than her tempting body. She pulled emotions—wants and desires—he'd never experienced.

He'd never entertained the idea of forever before Sadie. And to think he'd almost not come to Miami.

He didn't have to leave town while his crew renovated

his new place because one of his holiday rentals was between tenants and he'd taken it off the market indefinitely.

A mix up with some supplies had almost waylaid him except Nash, his construction manager, had assured Alex he'd take care of it. And it had been ages since he'd caught up with the guys from college and with everyone flying in from all over the country for John's birthday he hadn't wanted to miss out.

The only one missing was Alec Dane.

And thank God he was.

If his friend had been at the club last night, then Sadie wouldn't have come home with him. Probably wouldn't have mistaken them.

Alex had to thank whatever higher being was looking out for him because without the missing Alec or Sadie's lack of eyewear, he might have missed the best thing to ever happen to him.

He glanced down. She slept in his embrace, completely relaxed, and Alex lifted the glasses that were now sitting lopsided on her face. Sadie mumbled but didn't wake and he folded them, placed them on the pillow beside his head.

He couldn't reach the bedside table without moving her and he wanted them close for when she woke. She wanted to see him clearly this time and he'd make sure she saw every inch of him before the night was over.

He'd give her a few minutes of sleep before he woke her up. As much as he wanted to let her rest, he didn't want to waste one minute of their time together tonight.

If he told her he lived in Winter Lake and couldn't

convince her to keep seeing him once she moved there, tonight would be all he had, and he'd be damned if he wasn't going to use every second to make his mark on her so deep that when he showed up next week on her doorstep, she'd be thrilled to see him.

He trailed a hand down her back, the other up into her hair. She was soft and silky all over and Alex thought if he had a lifetime to touch her, it wouldn't be enough.

Squeezing his eyes shut, he took a deep breath and did something he couldn't ever recall doing before.

He prayed.

Prayed she let him into her life.

Prayed she wouldn't be angry when she worked out he'd lied by omission.

And prayed she didn't think he was some weird fucker who was stalking her when he knocked on her door.

He would tell her now if he thought it would do any good, except he was damn sure she'd agreed to come home with him again because she thought they'd never see each other after tomorrow morning.

Sadie stirred, lifted her head. "Oh. I fell asleep."

Her rumpled hair and sleepy gaze made him smile. "Yes, but not for long."

She pushed off and laid beside him. "I wasn't planning on sleeping at all tonight."

Alex grinned. It seemed they were on the same page. The 'make the most of every second they had tonight' page. "Let's take a shower."

"What?" She blinked then squinted at him when he climbed over her.

"Shower." He grabbed her hand and tugged. "I want you wet."

"Together?" Her hand trembled in his and he didn't miss the shiver that shook her breasts.

"Oh yeah. Definitely together."

Alex led the way to the bathroom and quickly turned on the water and maneuvered Sadie into the shower. He was glad there was plenty of room for the two of them. Then again, he didn't plan on giving her much space.

"Um, I..."

Alex grabbed the soap and lathered his hands. "Here." He handed the bar to Sadie.

"What—?" He slid his slick hands over her chest, soaping her breasts and nipples. "*Oh,*" she breathed out, her back arching toward him.

She shivered in spite of the warm water rushing over them, making him smile. Before the bubbles were washed away, he made sure to clean every inch of her chest. "Need more soap."

"A-are you g-going to wash all of m-me?"

"It's the least I can do seeing how I'm the one who got you all dirty." He winked.

"Oh. O-okay." She licked her lips and Alex's heart sped up, his cock twitching as hot blood filled it. "Do I g-get a t-turn?"

He knew her stammer was back due to nerves. Nervous anticipation was the good kind, and he planned to make her so tight with expectation, so on-edge that she begged. "Later."

Soap in hand, he dropped to his knees at her feet and started from the ground up. One leg at a time.

First her delicate foot and ankle, then up a slender calf to the sensitive spot behind her knee. Up the outside of her thigh, around the back to the crease where leg met ass.

Sadie trembled. She moaned. She gasped.

Then he started all over again on the other side.

By the time he'd reached the top of her left leg and palmed both ass cheeks, she was begging. Thank God.

His plan to drive her mad with desire hadn't included taking himself there too. It seemed giving Sadie pleasure ramped up his own need.

And he was sweating and shaking and cursing himself for a fool for not having the forethought to bring a condom into the bathroom with them.

She reached for him. "Alex."

He was done. Scooping her up, he turned and barely turned the shower off before charging out of the bathroom and back to bed.

They rolled, each fighting for control in their desperation to take that final plunge.

Alex wasn't sure how he managed it, but he sheathed his straining cock, pinned Sadie beneath him, and in one driving thrust, he impaled her on his entire length.

"Yes!"

Her cry echoed in his ears, throbbing to the beat of his heart as he surged in and out of her tight pussy.

She wrapped her legs around his waist, clawed at his back with her nails, and together they fell blindly into the most shattering climax of his life.

CHAPTER 17

Alex didn't need to open his eyes to know Sadie was gone.

He opened them anyway.

Except this time the day didn't stretch out bleak and empty before him.

He had a plan, and the first step was to pack his bags and catch an earlier flight home.

He had a lot to organize before Sadie arrived in Winter Lake.

CHAPTER 18

SADIE JERKED when the buzzer sounded. She still wasn't used to the sound, but then, she'd been daydreaming.

Again.

With a sigh, she pushed up off the floor and walked to the small intercom near the front door. "Hello?"

"Delivery for Sadie Emerson."

"That's me. Bring it up." She hit the door-release button and then opened the loft door.

The sound of footsteps echoed up the stairwell until a UPS driver came into view. He held a small box, and for the life of her, she couldn't remember ordering anything.

"Sign here." He held out an electronic gadget and she quickly scribbled her signature. "Thanks. Have a great day," he said as he handed her the package.

"Thank you." She flipped it over, looking for a clue as to its origin as she closed the door. "That's weird. No return address."

Making her way to the kitchen, she rummaged in the debris on the counter looking for her box cutter until she remembered having it in the bedroom last. Grabbing a knife, she sliced through the packing tape on the top and opened the flaps.

Staring at the bar of soap, Sadie's mouth dropped open. "Oh my God."

She pulled the soap out and saw the envelope underneath. She dropped the soap back in the box then opened the envelope. One sheet of folded paper was all it held.

Sadie,
Think of me while you unpack.
Love, Alex

She laughed. She didn't need a bar of soap or a note to think of Alex while she unpacked.

All she'd done since leaving him before dawn Sunday morning was think of him. No matter how many times she told herself it was over and done or how many mornings she woke without him beside her, she couldn't erase him from her mind.

He was the first thing she thought of when she woke. The last thought before sleep took her.

He starred in her dreams—day and night.

For three days she'd caught herself looking at every guy with the same colored hair, same height, thinking it was Alex. Except he was hundreds of miles away. Where she'd left him. In Miami.

Her mind had been playing tricks on her since she'd left

him sleeping in his bed. Just this morning she thought she'd seen him down the street when she'd ventured out for coffee.

His gift made her smile. It made her shiver. And it did nothing to help her forget him or their time together.

Sleeping with Alex had been a mistake. The best kind. She'd do it again in a heartbeat, even though she knew leaving would be torture. Knew that after only two nights he'd left a mark so deep, so permanent—like the tattoo on his back—that she'd never get over him.

She sighed and placed the note in the box on top of the soap. She'd put them in her room, in the back of the closet...

Oh, who was she trying to kid? The note would go on her bedside table where she could see it all the time and the soap would go in the shower where she'd... She shivered.

Sadie leaned against the counter and glanced around the room. Boxes sat in various stages of being unpacked, the picture she'd picked up in the little shop she'd come across yesterday afternoon leaned against the wall waiting to be hung. There was so much to do but suddenly she needed to get out. Walk in the fresh air and clear her mind.

As much as she loved her new place, it wasn't what she wanted. Not anymore. And that was Alex's fault too.

Before he'd talked about fences and houses and kids, she'd never even entertained the idea of a family—a husband.

Now all she could think about was getting married and

having children. Living in a big house with a huge yard where a dog chased the kids around.

And imagining Alex in that cozy picture was all too easy.

"Argh." She pushed off the counter and headed for the bathroom and a shower.

She'd get cleaned up and go out for an early dinner. There were plenty of restaurants in the area she could try. Just because she wouldn't be sharing the meal with Alex didn't mean she couldn't enjoy it.

Determined to forget Alex for a little while—she wasn't stupid enough to think she could forget about him completely—she showered and dressed.

She left the bedroom and grabbed her bag from the hook next to the front door. Sadie was fairly sure it was for coats but it suited her to hang her bag from it for now.

Once winter arrived she'd hang her coat there too. After she bought one of course. Miami winters didn't call for a thick jacket. She had no doubt Winter Lake would require a snow jacket.

Sliding open the big steel panel that was her front door, she felt lighter than she had in three days. No more moping around with Alex on her mind. He was her past and Winter Lake—her new job—was her future.

CHAPTER 19

ALEX SPOTTED Sadie as she came around the side of her place. He'd waited a couple of days before making any form of contact and he'd gone with sending a gift he thought she'd find funny as well as reminding her of what they had done their last night together.

Of course, he'd been determined to stay away for another day but Sadie was irresistible. He had to see her. Except she was heading out.

He was about half a block behind her as she made her way down Fire Trail Drive and onto Lake Front. Luckily for him she hadn't once looked behind her. Following at a distance he watched her stop at a couple of restaurants, reading their menus before moving on.

She hadn't reached the halfway point of Lake Front when she entered a little Italian place that was a recent addition to town and served great food.

Letting her go in, he waited a few minutes before

picking up his pace and entering the family owned restaurant.

In a lot of ways the place reminded Alex of Emilio's, where they had their one and only date. Not that Sadie would agree with that label. He grinned as he scanned the tables.

She was sitting in the far corner looking right at him like she'd seen a ghost. Alex waved and headed in her direction as though they'd arranged to meet here.

He pulled out the chair beside her and planted a quick kiss on her gaping mouth before taking a seat.

"Alex?" Her voice was strangled, like someone had hold of her vocal cords.

"Sadie." He grinned.

"H-how? W-where?" She shook her head. "*Alex?*"

"Did ya miss me?"

"Yes. No!" She crossed her arms over her chest. "Are you s-stalking me?"

Alex burst out laughing. If only she knew. "No. But I have a confession. Two, actually."

She glared at him.

"Let's order dinner first. We'll talk while we eat."

"Alex." Sadie growled his name through clenched teeth. Her show of anger didn't have the desired effect though—he thought she looked cute all riled up.

"Baby." He leaned in, brushed his mouth against her ear. "I promise to explain everything over dinner."

"Not before you tell me how you got my address."

Alex sighed. "Fine. Mel." He went with the small white lie and picked up a menu. Mel had given him the address but he'd known exactly where Sadie would be living when she'd described it to him at dinner Saturday night.

From his peripheral vision he watched Sadie's mouth open and shut several times before she huffed out a breath. "Damn her."

"Are you that unhappy to see me?" he asked.

Her gaze darted to meet his. "I...that is..." She sighed and slumped back in her chair. "No."

"Then let's order and we can talk."

"Fine. But I want to know why you're here before the food arrives." She reached for her menu. Barely glimpsed at it before saying, "I'll have the fettuccini carbonara."

"Good choice. I think I'll join you." He signaled the waiter they were ready to order.

The teenager took their order and the menus and hadn't even turned away when Sadie was on Alex. And not in a good way.

"Why are you here? Here in Winter Lake, New York, and *here*," she indicated the table, "right where I am."

Where to start... "I live in Winter Lake."

Her eyes grew huge behind her glasses and her mouth hung open. "B-but..."

"I was visiting John for a couple of days. I lived in New York City for a few years after college then when I opened my own business I based it here. Actually, I grew up here. My parents still live in the house they bought when they got married."

"You're from Winter Lake? Winter Lake, New York, as in here"—she waved a hand toward the front door of the restaurant—"Winter Lake?"

He nodded.

"Wow."

The waiter arrived with their drinks, placed them on the table, and left without a word.

"Okay." Sadie took a sip of her soda. "So you're from here and you still live here."

"Yep. Except for my time in college and the two years after that."

"And where exactly is that? Where you live now?" she asked, her eyes narrowed.

Alex had always gotten off on Sadie's brain as much as her body, and she was using the former right now to come to her own conclusions. He figured she'd be close to the truth with her deductions.

"You live near me, don't you?"

He smiled.

"Lord." She closed her eyes briefly before fixing him with a hard look. "So when I told you where I'd be living you knew exactly, probably to the building, where I was talking about. Mel didn't need to rat me out at all, did she?"

Shaking his head, he said, "No, she didn't. Our streets are parallel to each other, my place is one street back from yours. In fact it was my company that renovated your loft and the space below it."

She sat up as though someone had rammed a steel rod up her spine. "You live on the street behind mine?"

"I do."

"And you didn't think to tell me?"

"I did."

"But you didn't."

"No. I didn't because you took off before I woke up. Again." He covered her hand with his. "Sadie, I wanted more time with you. I still do. But I also didn't want to spook you at all and we both know that going home with me, twice, was already freaking you out."

She opened her mouth then snapped it shut without a word.

"I have a suggestion," he offered.

She scowled. "I'm not going home with you."

Alex laughed. He noticed the corner of Sadie's mouth twitching as if she were holding back a smile and he leaned over and kissed her.

"Go out with me. Let me show you this town. Give us both time to see where this thing goes. Because, Sadie, this is bigger than anything I've ever felt and I'm not about to let it slip away without taking it as far as I can."

"I don't know—"

"Don't decide yet. Let's just enjoy dinner and worry about the rest later." He smiled and leaned back as the waiter delivered their meals.

Sadie stared at him for what felt like forever before picking up her fork and spearing it into her pasta. "Okay. Dinner. Then we'll see."

Alex grinned. He'd take what he could get and push for more when she let her guard down. He knew he could use their off-the-charts chemistry to convince her except he wanted to prove to her that they were more than just hot sex.

Keeping his hands off her would be hard and chances were good he'd probably slip up more than once over the next few days. As long as she gave them a shot, he'd be happy. And his aim was to convince her to give them a chance by the time she went to work Monday morning.

Four days.

He had tonight and four full days to show her his town and convince her they were worth more than a two-night stand.

CHAPTER 20

SADIE STARED out at the twinkling lights, awestruck by the beauty of Winter Lake and the mountains surrounding it. She was so glad Alex had talked her into a trip up to the lookout tonight in spite of not wanting to hike in the dark.

The view was spectacular. She could see the whole town from here. She'd checked out everything thoroughly, and Alex had pointed out her loft and the building her office was located in, as well as too many other landmarks to remember.

She'd definitely be coming back up here. In daylight next time. That way she would be able to see the mountains that were too dark to see now.

A gust of wind blew hard enough to make her wobble on her feet and she shivered as the cold air rushed over her.

Alex's arms slipped around her from behind. "Cold? Want to go back down now?"

They'd been out in the elements, almost two thousand

feet above sea level, for more than an hour and Sadie still wasn't ready to leave. "No. I'm fine. It's a bit chilly but I don't want to give up this view yet."

He chuckled in her ear, his lips brushing her skin as he murmured, "You live in Winter Lake now. You can come up any day or night you want."

A smile curled her mouth. "I can, can't I?" She turned her head to see him and her glasses bumped his jaw. "Oops. Sorry."

"No problem."

"I should really try to get used to wearing contacts more."

"Why? I like your sexy red glasses." He grinned and dropped a kiss on her forehead.

She shivered again. This time it had nothing to do with the cold breeze.

Alex thought her glasses were sexy? And here she'd thought they made her look like the bookworm she was. She'd gone with the red frames in the hope of appearing more sophisticated and less nerdy, and if Alex was to be believed, the choice had worked in a completely different way.

"C'mon. There's a place down on Lake Front that serves the best hot chocolate."

Alex released her and took her hand. Entwining his fingers with hers, he pulled her away from the lookout edge and toward the trail. Glancing back over her shoulder, Sadie took one more look at Winter Lake.

"I'll bring you back again," he said with a chuckle.

She turned to find Alex watching her with a grin. "It's

so pretty but I think I want to come back during the day next time. I bet you can see for miles."

He nodded as he pulled her beside him and wrapped an arm around her waist, tucking her into his side and his warmth. "You can. How's tomorrow work for you? We can go up Hargrove Trail to Fire Trail Ridge too. It's a different view from that side of the lake."

"Yes!" Excitement bubbled through her. "I want to see it all!"

Throwing his head back, Alex laughed and squeezed her closer. "Relax. You've got the rest of your life to explore the area."

Swallowing, Sadie tried to corral some of the exhilaration threatening to burst out. A deep breath gave her another second to calm down but she still couldn't keep the excited thrill from her voice. "I can't wait that long!"

He stopped walking and pulled her around to face him, placed his hands on her shoulders, and dropped his head so they were eye to eye. "I promise I'll show you everything but it'll take longer than you think. You have to see everything in all the seasons. If you think the lake looks good now, wait until you see it frozen and everyone grabs their skates."

"Oh! I've always wanted to skate on a frozen lake. Not much chance of that in Miami and the indoor rink isn't the same. I want the sky above me, the wind on my face, the trees surrounding me..."

"You'll have to wait a few months for that." He smiled and lowered his head until their mouths almost touched. "I promise to take you there as soon as they set it up."

"Really?"

She bounced on her toes, acting like a kid at Christmas, but she'd dreamed of living in a small town for as long as she could remember. A place where you didn't nod at strangers in the grocery store or the gas station because they weren't strangers.

And now she was here.

With Alex.

The whole thing seemed surreal.

He tweaked her nose. "I'll show you everything there is to see in Winter Lake."

"I'm going to hold you to that." She smiled and slid her arms around his waist bringing their mouths even closer; her stomach fluttered, her body tightened.

A memory of Alex pressing her to the wall and kissing her senseless in the elevator in Miami flashed through her mind. Heat washed over her and twisted low in her pelvis, making her sex clench.

They—*she*—needed a distraction or she'd be pushing him against the nearest tree and begging him to kiss her. "So where is this hot chocolate you raved about?"

"It's on the other side of town from your place. Do you mind walking? It's a bit of a hike from here but I can give you the tour guide spiel along the way."

"Sounds perfect," she said as she stepped back and pulled out of Alex's arms. There was only so much temptation a woman could take and his lips were proving very tempting right now.

She sucked in a breath as Alex pulled her back and snuggled her into his side. The cool night air swirled around them, the light on Alex's jacket pocket making it easy to see the trail leading back to the edge of the lake near the end of town.

Burrowing in closer, she soaked in Alex's warmth. She'd worn a lightweight sweater that didn't stand up to the cool spring weather of the mountains. There was a shopping trip in her future.

She'd definitely need warmer clothes before next winter. Everything she had was for Miami's warmer weather. Obviously those clothes offered no protection against colder northern temperatures.

"Here." Alex freed himself from her grip and took off his leather jacket. "Put this on."

"Oh, no. You'll freeze in just a t-shirt. I'll be fine." She tried to hide the shiver that vibrated her jaw, almost rattling her teeth. Sadie frowned when he smiled at her indulgently and held his jacket out for her.

"Just put it on. My mother would kill me if she knew I wore a jacket while my date froze to death."

"This isn't a date," she grumbled as she turned and slipped her arms into the warm sleeves. The scent of leather and Alex surrounded her, instantly enveloping her in comfort.

"She'd still kill me." Alex spun her around and zipped her up to the chin, turning up the collar to shield her neck. "There. Better. Now let's get that hot chocolate and warm you up on the inside too."

Sadie could think of a few ways to warm up on the inside except she wasn't supposed to go there. She shouldn't even be *here*. When she'd walked out on a sleeping Alex Sunday morning, she'd planned to leave him in the past.

However, it appeared as though Alex didn't want to be left behind.

In fact, he was doing everything he could to stay in her present *and* her future. Promising to show her the town—take her skating when the lake froze over.

How could she get over him if he was always in her face?

Always there to remind her of their attraction? Of how good it felt to be with him, and she wasn't just referring to the bedroom either.

He had a sharp mind. A great sense of humor—it was a little offbeat but highly amusing. And yes, he was good in bed. But the biggest draw to Alex was the way he made her feel.

Without cheesy lines or over-the-top compliments, he made her feel comfortable, relaxed, happy.

Appreciated.

She felt important. Worthy of his attention and time.

With all that in mind Sadie had no clue why she thought not seeing Alex was a good idea, or the right choice. It certainly wasn't what she wanted.

She sighed and leaned her head against his shoulder. His arm around her tightened and snuggled her closer to his side.

"Hey. You okay?" he asked. "If you're cold, we can grab my truck and drive."

"No. I'm all right." Sadie tipped her head back to look

at him. "I guess all the unpacking is starting to catch up with me though. I'm a little tired."

"Bake And Brew is at the end of Lake Front. We'll grab our hot chocolate to go then head home if you're too tired to stay." He dropped a kiss on her forehead.

Sadie closed her eyes and breathed deep. Alex surrounded her. His warmth, his smell, his comforting embrace. Opening her eyes, she stared at the trail in front of them.

It didn't matter that she'd told herself she shouldn't see Alex again because her body wanted the opposite—and Sadie was beginning to think her heart might too.

CHAPTER 21

ALEX DIDN'T KNOW what happened, only that something had changed.

In the last few minutes Sadie had gone very quiet and tucked herself against him as though she feared he'd disappear in a puff of smoke.

He wanted to ask what was wrong, except given how shaky the ground was between them, he didn't think he should. He'd already pushed his luck a number of times today, as well as the numerous times since he'd run into her at the club in Miami last Friday.

Was that really less than a week ago?

Five days. And they'd had less than half that time together.

Not nearly long enough to be thinking the things he was thinking.

Except he couldn't deny any of those feelings, couldn't

ignore the wants and desires surrounding the woman in his arms.

He might be zooming ahead at mach fifty billion but it didn't mean she was.

The sensible thing to do would be to back off.

He'd let her get her bearings while continuing with his get-to-know-each-other campaign without pressuring for more than she was ready to give, and hopefully she'd come to the same conclusion he had.

They were more than two nights of hot sex.

More than a couple of old friends catching up, hooking up, and hanging out.

He knew that to his bone marrow.

Sadie just had to catch up.

"Here we are." He guided her into Bake And Brew, which, in his opinion, served the best hot chocolate in the country. "Hey, Carly, two specials to go, thanks."

"First-name-basis with the girl behind the counter." Sadie glanced up at him. "That usually means you come here often or—"

Alex pressed his fingers to her mouth. "Don't finish that thought."

She eyed him with one cocked brow.

"C'mon." He pulled her closer to the counter where Carly was making their drinks. "Carly, this is Sadie. She's new in town. Sadie, Carly Murdock, my cousin."

"Oh." The pink in Sadie's cheeks deepened.

He bent down and placed his mouth near her ear. "Yeah. *Oh.*"

He smiled when he stood straight. She seemed to have a misconception about him and women. He'd set her straight. Telling her wouldn't do any good. He'd have to show her.

"Nice to meet you, Sadie. How do you know Alex?" Carly expertly steamed milk while keeping her full attention on Sadie. "You're not in the building game are you?"

"What? No. I'm in finance. I start a new job on the Economic Development Board next week."

"I hate numbers. Have to say, my accountant hates them too when I walk into his office with a shoebox full of receipts." Carly laughed.

Sadie shuddered. "Please tell me you're talking about your personal expenses and not your business accounts."

"Ah..." Carly held up a bowl of marshmallows and waggled it in front of them. "Yes? No?"

Sadie laughed. "Yes, please."

"So, how do you know each other?" Carly asked.

"College," Alex answered. And to deflect further cross-examination, which he knew was coming because this was Carly, he asked, "How's Mac?"

His cousin frowned. And was that a growl? "No comment."

Alex laughed. "What did he do this time?"

"What didn't he do more like it." Carly handed over their drinks. "On the house."

"Hey. No." He pulled out his wallet.

"Alex, you send more customers my way than any form of advertising I've ever taken out. I can afford to shout you and Sadie."

He scowled. "I don't do it for freebies." He took a ten from his wallet and dropped it in the tip jar.

"I know, I know." She leaned over the counter and, grabbing his shirt, yanked him in and planted a kiss on his cheek. "I still owe you."

"Nonsense. You'd do the same for me." Alex picked up a cup and handed it to Sadie. "I helped Carly get this place built out when she first bought it."

Sadie smiled at him. "And I bet you only charged her for the materials."

"Ha!" Carly smirked. "She so has your number."

"Hmm..." Alex sipped his hot chocolate and contemplated Carly's words.

Sadie did know him in some ways. The question was, did she know enough to give him—them—a chance?

Carly came out from behind the counter. "I'll lock up after you. Not that I'm pushing you out the door."

Alex glanced at his watch. "You're closing up late." He hadn't even thought about the time before now. It was unusual for Carly to be open after nine on a Wednesday night."

"Yeah. Grady and a few of his teammates were here. You just missed them."

"Grady's in town?" Alex slipped his hand into Sadie's free one.

"I think they came up this afternoon." Carly followed them to the door. "It was lovely to meet you, Sadie. Don't be a stranger."

"Oh, I won't. Not after I've sampled your hot chocolate." Sadie smiled.

"Told you it was the best." Alex gave her hand a quick squeeze. "Wait until you try her baked goods. I don't know what she does to her cinnamon rolls but they're the best I've ever tasted, and I've tasted plenty. And don't get me started on her chocolate chip cookies or her—"

"Oh, you." Carly gave him a push out the door. "Get out of here."

He waited to hear the deadbolt slide home behind them.

Hot drinks in hand, Alex led Sadie back down the street.

"You still okay to walk?" he asked as he tucked her against his side and tried to protect her from the worst of the wind that had picked up since they'd been inside Bake And Brew.

Sadie yawned.

Alex laughed. "Okay, my place for my truck." He kept her snug against him and led her through an alley that crossed through several of the streets parallel to Lake Front.

His place was probably only a few minutes closer to Bake And Brew than Sadie's but it *was* closer which meant he could get her out of the cold quicker and by the time he got her home she'd be warm and he'd be satisfied he hadn't frozen her to death.

It took under five minutes to reach his house and he wasted no time unlocking his truck and getting Sadie inside. As soon as the engine turned over, he cranked up the heat and pointed all the vents in her direction.

"It'll only take a second to warm up."

"It's not so bad now we're out of the wind." Seatbelt buckled, she wrapped both hands around her cup. "I'll have to get some warmer clothes sooner than later. I researched the weather and thought I'd have more time. It's way colder than I thought it would be for late spring."

"There's a place on Lake Front, Winter Lake Wears—it stocks everything you'll need to make it through the cooler mountain temperatures. They have an extensive winter clothing selection. They'll have what you need to make it through next winter."

"Great, I thought I'd have to go to Saratoga Springs."

"Nope. We've got everything you need right here." He wanted to add everything included him but held his tongue.

One step at a time.

Right now, in spite of the temptation to follow her inside when they reached her place he wouldn't. He'd prove to himself—and hopefully Sadie—that his intentions were about more than getting her into bed.

She stifled another yawn and leaned her head back against the seat. "God. Why am I suddenly so tired?"

"You've had a busy week."

"I have." She shifted, turned toward him. "And it's not finished. I'm not finished. God, there's so much to unpack. I don't remember owning this much stuff."

"Need some help? I'm good for lifting heavy things." Alex raised an arm and flexed his muscles.

Sadie laughed. "I'm sure you are, but I'm good. It's just unpacking boxes. Lots and lots of boxes."

"The offer stands." He pulled up in front of Sadie's

place and reached over to stop her from hopping out. "Wait there. I'll come around."

"You don't—"

"Nope. My mother would—"

She held up a hand. "I'm seeing a pattern here."

"Wait until you meet my mom; you'll get it." He grinned and popped his door. Racing around the front of the truck, he reached Sadie's door just as she opened it. "I asked you to wait."

"I'm perfectly capable of opening a car door and climbing out." Her bottom lip protruded in an adorable little pout.

Alex couldn't resist. He leaned in and placed a kiss on that perfect mouth.

She gasped, her lips parting, enticing him to take them deeper. It was another thing he couldn't resist.

Slipping his tongue into her mouth, he swallowed her moan as she melted into him. Alex didn't understand how her surrender could be a demand.

A demand for more.

A car whizzed past and cold air rushed around them. They jerked apart. Sadie's eyes widened behind her lopsided glasses, her breath coming in short, sharp bursts and her cheeks a pretty shade of pink.

He wanted to dive right back in again.

"Oh God." Sadie scrambled out of the truck and moved away from him.

An awkward silence settled over them as he shut the door and turned to join her on the sidewalk. Gripping her elbow, he guided her around the side of the old converted store house to her front door.

The place had been turned into two living spaces. The bottom level had three bedrooms, two and a half baths, and a combination kitchen-living space. Upstairs, reached through a separate entrance, was an open loft with one separate bedroom designed for holiday renting.

It had been one of Alex's first jobs when he'd moved home and he still loved the concept even if he would prefer Sadie live with him. That would never happen if he kept jumping forward. Kept rushing.

Kissing her had pushed things firmly back into the sex zone and while he wanted that, wanted more sex with Sadie, he wanted other things too.

He wanted to hang out like they had tonight, he wanted to know what her favorite food was, her favorite movie. Would she like the winter months or would she hate being snowed in?

So much to learn, so much to discover.

He wanted it all with Sadie. He just had to get her to start down the path he was already on.

First he had to get them back to the comfortable, easy way they were before they'd gotten carried away with a kiss.

The incident proved one thing though. Their chemistry was explosive. It took the smallest of sparks to set them both blazing out of control.

If he didn't leave now, he wouldn't.

"Got your key?" he asked.

"Oh. Yes." Sadie dug into the front pocket of her jeans and pulled out a single key. No ring.

Alex took it from her and unlocked the door. Handing the key back, he said, "I had a great night," as he urged her inside.

"I...yes, me too." She smiled at him, her lips a little wobbly and unsure.

He leaned forward and gave her a quick peck on the mouth. "See you tomorrow."

Before she could say anything else, Alex nudged her farther inside and closed the door between them.

Smiling, he shoved his hands in his pockets to stop himself from opening the door again. When he heard the deadbolt slide home, he turned and walked back to his truck.

And if he walked like the hounds of hell were nipping at his heels, it was because they were hounds.

His own personal lust hounds with the jagged teeth of a need so sharp they sliced him raw.

CHAPTER 22

SADIE TURNED over with a groan and rolled right off the mattress, hitting the floor with a bone-jarring thud. "Shit!"

The buzzer echoed through the loft again.

"Dammit." Pushing to her knees, she moaned and got to her feet. She hoped her glasses hadn't been knocked off the bedside table—the one that didn't require assembly.

Finding them where she'd left them, she slipped them on and blinked the world into focus.

Eyeing the scattered pieces of timber that made up her bed lying around the room, she wondered if maybe she should have taken Alex up on his offer to help.

Of course she hadn't expected it to be that hard to put a bedframe together. Then again, she'd also expected DIY furniture to come with the necessary tools to assemble it.

Obviously not.

The buzzer sounded again except this time whoever it was kept the stupid thing pressed down.

"I'm coming," she yelled. Why, was anyone's guess, when the person ringing her bell was a floor below and would never hear her.

Stumbling on her sleep groggy legs, Sadie made her way to the intercom. "Yeah?"

"Sadie. It's me. Alex."

As if she needed him to tell her who it was. Her body had instantly reacted to the sound of his deep voice. She shuddered as muscles clenched and her panties grew moist. "Why are you here?"

He'd left her at her door last night a little confused and with no way of contacting him. Sure, he knew where she lived, but other than his *our places are a street apart* she had no clue how to find Alex.

Okay fine, she could probably recognize it if she walked down his street.

"I brought you some coffee."

Oh God. Magic words. She pressed the button to unlock the downstairs door, then slid open the loft door.

Glancing down at herself, she couldn't find the energy to care that she was dressed in a pair of threadbare sweatpants, one of her old oversized college football jerseys and a pair of odd socks because her feet had gotten cold during the night and they were all she could find. And no doubt her hair looked like she'd stuck her finger in an electrical outlet.

Running her hands over her head, she sighed. Too late to do anything about her state now. She could hear Alex coming up the stairs.

"Morning." His smile was bright and his eyes sparkled and he just about bounced on his feet.

She grimaced and reached for the cup he held out toward her. "Are you one of *those* people?" she muttered in disgust.

"What people?" Alex sipped at his own coffee.

"A morning person." She looked around. "What time is it anyway?"

"Seven."

"Seven?" she screeched.

Alex cringed. "Ah, yeah, is that a problem?" His gaze trailed down to her odd sock-covered feet. "*Oh shit.* Did I wake you?"

Sadie narrowed her eyes and wondered what might be the best way to commit murder. There was certainly plenty of isolated mountain areas to hide a body.

"I thought for sure you'd be up by now. I've been up since five."

"Five?" she croaked, murder looking better by the second. "I think I may have still been awake at five."

"What? Why?"

She shrugged. "I was unpacking and time got away with me." She'd been so tired when Alex had dropped her off she figured she'd fall straight into bed, but the second she walked inside and remembered her bed wasn't put together yet, she'd set about getting it done. In the end she'd given up, made up the mattress on the floor, and collapsed on it.

Alex surveyed the room. "Okay. What can I help you with?"

"Don't you have a job or something?" Surely he couldn't spend the day—in the middle of the week—helping her.

"I was on the job at five-thirty. My construction manager has everything under control for now."

"Construction manager?" Sadie took a sip of her coffee and discovered it was exactly the way she liked it. Right down to the shot of hazelnut. She took another—bigger—sip and moaned, her eyes drifting shut. "Mmm...this is good."

Alex made a choking sound that had her eyes popping wide and her fight-or-flight instinct kicking in. Her heart raced and she was reaching for him without thought.

"Are you—"

"Yes," he gulped air. "Went down the wrong hole."

He wouldn't look at her so she ducked and bobbed until she could see his face clearly. "Are you sure?" He was still breathing choppily.

Alex nodded. "Yeah." He cleared his throat. Gave her a small grin. "I'm good."

Sadie wasn't sure why she thought he was lying except she did. With his breathing steady and the smile on his face growing wider she let it go and took another sip of heaven. "God this is either really good because I was up most of the night or it's just really good."

"I picked it up at Bake And Brew."

"Ah, that explains it. Carly knows her stuff." In the two days she'd been in Winter Lake she hadn't ventured that far down Lake Front. She'd been making do with the sludge that the servo offered each morning. If only she'd known what awaited her farther down the street.

"Have you eaten?" He held up a hand. "Wait. Of course you haven't. I woke you up. Why don't I go out and grab something for breakfast, then we can get stuck in here and finish off your unpacking. With the two of us pitching in, we should have it done in no time, then I can take you on another tour of Winter Lake."

Sadie wasn't about to look a gift horse in the mouth. "Do you have a tool kit?"

One of his eyebrows arched. "Definitely."

"Excellent. This way." She turned and led the way to the bedroom. "I have no idea what you'll actually need but if you can get this put together for me, I'll forever be in your debt."

"Wow." Alex stood in the doorway beside her. "Um... did the box this came in blow up?"

"Ha ha." She took another fortifying gulp of coffee. "I thought it would come with the tools to put it together."

"Right. Here." He handed her his cup. "I'll duck down to my truck and get my toolbox. Be back in a minute."

"Take the key off the table by the door. I'll grab a quick shower while you're gone."

Alex's nostrils flared and he took a step closer. His eyes were black, his brown irises pushed out by the expanded pupils. He gave himself a shake and Sadie watched as the blaze of desire simmered down.

"Okay." His voice was strained, his jaw taut, but he'd gained control of the lust that had flashed through his eyes only moments ago.

She'd never seen anything like it. Never watched that closely when it came to men and the emotions they felt.

Alex was different though.

She wanted to know everything about him and that included his reactions to her.

He gulped, his Adam's apple bobbing violently. "I'll be back," he ground out before spinning on his heel and striding from the room.

Sadie stood still. Sucking in air and fighting against the urge to call him back. Ask him to join her in the shower.

Because if she was right, and she was pretty sure she was—she wasn't that clueless about men—that's precisely what he'd been thinking about doing.

CHAPTER 23

Alex ran out of there like his ass was on fire. Appropriate, considering it felt as if his balls were ablaze.

Damn. She'd been all rumpled and flushed from sleep and all he could think about was tumbling her back into bed and making her more rumpled and flushed.

He dragged a hand down his face and jogged over to his truck. Those burning balls hurt with each step he took but he figured by the time he reached the truck the hard-on above them would have disappeared.

Maybe.

Sadie had him semi-hard twenty-four-seven.

He couldn't remember having this many erections as a teenager. No wonder he couldn't think straight. His blood was permanently pooled in his groin.

Reaching the truck, he glanced into the bed and cursed. He'd left his tools at the house across the lake.

Dammit. He'd have to go grab some from the worksite down on Lake Front.

Jumping in the truck, he drove like a madman and hoped he didn't get pulled over, and if he did it would be his cousin Laura. At least then he'd stand a chance of getting out of a ticket.

He didn't bother parking in a designated spot in the lot beside the building site; instead he stopped behind two of his company's trucks and left the motor running.

"Hey, boss. Back already?" Nash called out from the rear door of the two-story shop they were renovating.

"Just need some tools," he explained as he followed Nash inside.

Alex let his site manager go up the stairs to the second floor without engaging him further. He didn't want to get into a conversation with anyone as to why he needed tools. He'd rather grab them and get back to Sadie's before she had a chance to get out of the shower.

It might be a little masochistic but Alex wanted to be there while she was in the bathroom. He shook his head. Lord, he was in deep if just knowing she was naked and wet was enough to get him off.

He slowed his steps. Maybe it was better if she finished before he got back. If the *thought* of her naked, wet body had him sweating and his heart racing, not to mention his cock attempting to impersonate Houdini and get out of his pants, then being in her loft while she actually was wet and naked would test his control to its limit.

Taking his time, Alex walked through the lower level. Other than a good clean, the place was good to go. The ground floor had been finished a week prior and the owner had already been by and was thrilled with the results. Now she just had to wait for the second floor to be completed.

He spotted a toolbox in the corner of the back room that would become the office of the yoga studio when it opened. Upstairs would be living space for the owner as well as some specialty treatment rooms. He didn't have a clue what kind of treatments, he only knew the fittings the owner had requested.

Rummaging through the tools, he decided he'd take the whole thing instead of attempting to pick out what he'd need. Better to have it all on hand than have to race back for something else.

"Nash?" he called up the stairs. "I'm heading back out."

"Okay, boss. I'll call you later with an update."

"Thanks." He headed out to his truck and smiled. There was no way you could leave the keys in, truck running, in either of the other two places he'd lived without it being stolen.

One more reason to love his home town. One more thing for Sadie to love. An almost zero crime rate.

Detouring past Bake And Brew, Alex picked up some fresh cinnamon rolls then drove back to Sadie's. When he used her key to enter the loft, he could hear the water running and knew any effort to get his wayward hormones under control had been wasted.

He sucked in a breath as his whole body went stiff with tension—the part between his legs the stiffest.

Alex figured if he didn't convince Sadie to move their relationship along soon he was bound to suffer some sort of injury. Either starving his brain of oxygen due to lack of blood flow or his cock would burst open like the walls of a flooded dam.

The water shut off and it took all of Alex's willpower to stay where he was. If he went into Sadie's bedroom now, all bets were off. There'd be no way he could stop himself from taking her to bed again.

He had to keep his ultimate goal in mind though. Aim for the end game instead of the initial skirmish. Sure, he'd score some points along the way, but if he rushed her now, he risked losing her before they really got started.

As far as Alex was concerned, this past weekend counted against him. He'd picked her up in a club. He hadn't even bought her a drink before asking her to go home with him.

There were extenuating circumstances. They knew each other from college and she was as into him as he was her, but his motives had been anything but pure that first night.

And the fact she'd mistaken him for someone else didn't sit well, even if she'd spent a second night with him knowing exactly who she was screwing.

"Oh. You're back." Sadie stood in the doorway of her room in a towel. Her hair hung wet around her shoulders, her skin glistened with the water dripping from the ends.

"Sadie." He growled her name, his hands clenching the bakery bag and toolbox. "Go into your room and shut the door."

"What?"

Alex wanted to laugh at the confused look on her face except he was too busy concentrating on staying put.

"Alex?" She took a step towards him.

She was going to kill him.

"Are you okay?"

Was he? Doubtful.

"Alex?" she raised her voice, as though he hadn't heard her the first time. He'd heard her all right. He saw her too.

He took a deep breath. Let it out slowly. "Sadie. If you don't put a closed, preferably locked, door between us in the next three seconds I'm going to lose control and strip that towel off you."

"Oh...I..." She took a step back. Stopped.

"Now."

She didn't move. In fact her gaze raked him, a corresponding fire to the one inside him flashing in her eyes.

Jesus Christ. "*Sadie.*" Fuck. He was begging.

Then she did something that blew his mind. And possibly his cock if the wetness suddenly coating the tip was any indication.

She let go of the towel.

CHAPTER 24

It was amazing how liberating one decision could be.

She was tired of going back and forth about Alex. She wanted him. It didn't matter what her brain said. Her body and heart were somehow linked to him and when he was around she felt incredible—as if she could accomplish anything and everything she'd ever wanted—could ever want.

"Sadie." He took a step toward her. He didn't rush her like she'd expected. The way he looked at her, his gaze traveling the length of her bare body, stopping in all the relevant spots for extra perusal, left her hot and shivery.

He stood there, gazing at her, for what seemed forever. She was surprised she didn't fidget or have the urge to cover up. With Alex, she wanted him to see all of her. She'd always been modest, shy about exposing her body to anyone, particularly men.

Although, other than Alex, there'd been only one guy she'd gotten naked with.

"Sadie, if I come any closer we're not putting your bed together anytime soon."

She smiled, an inner vixen she'd had no clue existed stepping out. "We don't need a bed."

"Be sure." He took another step, put the toolbox on top of an unpacked box, a white paper bag on top of that. "There's no going back."

Sadie nodded. "I know."

Alex was only a few feet away now. Almost touching distance. "I want it all. Everything."

Her throat constricted. Her heart pounded in her chest. His words were some kind of warning. A caution for her to be absolutely sure she wanted to do this.

Was she a fool to let him in? She knew with every breath she took Alex had the power to hurt her. Deeply. She was already a little in love with him. Maybe she was getting in over her head, except right now, with him staring at her, breathing hard, his body taut with restraint and her body flush with desire, she didn't care if she drowned in him.

"Sadie."

"I was supposed to be Dee." She'd failed so miserably at reinventing herself.

He grinned. "I remember. But like I said Friday night, I like Sadie. I like her a lot. Always have. I haven't changed my mind on that."

She tilted her head to keep her gaze connected with his. When had he moved so close? His heat touched her naked skin, sent shivers down her spine. "I wanted to fit in. Be sophisticated—confident."

"Sadie is all that and more." Alex brushed the backs of his fingers down her cheek, his gaze softening. "Look at you. You're bold and beautiful and funny and intelligent and everything I've ever wanted but never looked for."

"I..." She shook her head. She didn't feel any of those things.

"You're brave and determined."

"But—"

"And successful."

"I am?" She trembled as his fingers trailed down her throat.

"Yes." He bent toward her, pressed his mouth to hers in a barely there kiss. "That's the Sadie I see. The one I want."

"You do?"

"Definitely."

"I...*really?*"

Alex's lips curled against hers. "Really."

"So this is just sex?"

His smile turned devilish. "Oh, this is definitely that. And so much more."

Before she blinked, he had her off her feet, her naked body clasped to his fully clothed one. The roughness of his jeans excited her, just as the softness of his t-shirt rubbing across her nipples thrilled her.

He walked the short distance to her bed, holding her tight against his chest. He didn't speak. He didn't have to. The look in his eyes said a thousand things.

"Alex."

"Sadie." With a smile, he lowered her to the mattress. "We need to get your bed put together."

"What? No!" She wrapped her arms and legs around him, holding on tight.

Laughing, he said, "Don't worry. I didn't mean right now."

"Oh." She loosened her grip but didn't let go—couldn't.

"Right now we're going to see if we can't work up an appetite for the cinnamon rolls I bought."

"You bought cinnamon rolls?"

"Yeah, but you've gotta earn them first."

Sadie grinned. "I'm sure I can manage that." She slid one hand into his hair, tugged his head down, and pressed her mouth to his. Parting her lips, she thrust her tongue between his and probed deep.

Long seconds later, Alex lifted his head. "Oh yeah. There she is."

"Huh?"

"My Sadie."

"Your Sadie?" Had one of Alex's kisses finally blown her mind to smithereens? She had no idea what he was talking about.

"Bold. Confident. Determined. Not to mention sexy as hell when she takes charge." He brushed the hair from her forehead. "But you know what's the best part of you?"

"No. What?"

"That you're smart enough to recognize a good thing when you see it and brave enough to go after it."

"It took five margaritas to get that daring. And then I botched it up and made a mistake."

"I wouldn't call that a mistake, and that was only the first night. What's your excuse for the second one?"

"Ah..." She might be lying here naked with him on top of her but she wasn't about to reveal she'd been falling for him even then.

There was only so much vulnerability a girl could take.

CHAPTER 25

ALEX WATCHED emotions flicker through Sadie's eyes and decided to let her off the hook for now. He had her where he wanted her, after all. No point wrecking the moment by pushing her into a corner.

"You know, I think I like being your daring mistake." He nuzzled the skin beneath her ear and felt her shiver under him. Moving south, he licked his way down her throat to her collarbone. "Hmm...you smell good. Taste better."

"Alex."

He lifted his head, met her gaze. The need swirling in her eyes took his breath. "Sadie."

"I need..." She rocked her hips up into him, grinding her pussy on his length. "It's been too long."

It had been four days since he'd been inside her and she was right. It had been way too long.

Pushing up, he jumped to his feet and quickly stripped

out of his clothes. His jeans got hooked up on his boots and he hopped around until he fell on his ass beside her.

Laughing, Sadie got to her knees and helped him tug his feet free. He kicked his pants away and lunged for her. Giggling and squirming, she wrestled until she'd maneuvered him to his back and crawled on top of him.

"I don't have any condoms." She bit her bottom lip.

"I've got one in my wallet." He reached for his jeans, flipping them around until he found the back pocket. "We're fixing your lack of protection as soon as possible."

"I'm on the Pill."

Alex stilled. Swallowed. "What are you saying?"

She shrugged. "We can get tested. Not worry about condoms from now on."

His heart stopped. Dear God. He was dumbstruck—humbled. Trusting him to that level... "*Sadie*." Alex palmed her cheeks, pulled her face down to his. Kissed her softly.

"If you don't want to—"

"Baby, I'm in awe. That you would trust me that much..." He kissed her again. "I'll make an appointment today but I have a full physical yearly for work insurance. I'm clean. Plus I've never been with a woman without a condom."

Her smile wobbled. "I haven't either. Had sex without a condom, I mean."

Alex grinned. "Then it looks like we'll be experiencing that first together."

Sadie's smile steadied. "So..." She glanced at the packet in his hand.

"Wow. You don't want me to use this?"

She chewed on her bottom lip again and Alex reached up to dislodge it.

"You have no idea how much I love having your trust but we're going to do this right. We'll use these," he waggled the packet in his hand, "until we get checked out."

"Okay." She plucked the condom from his fingers and ripped it open. "Let's use it then."

Alex watched through hooded eyes as Sadie took care of protecting them then positioned herself over him.

She lowered onto him in slow increments and Alex held his breath, thought he'd explode if she didn't hurry. Even his hands on her hips, his fingertips digging in to urge her on, didn't speed her up.

"Sadie. You're killing me," he groaned. Moving his hands from her hips, he slid them up her ribs until he cupped her breasts. Weighing them in his palms, he stroked his thumbs across both nipples. "Move, baby. I need you to move."

"Pinch them."

"What?"

"My nipples. Pinch them." She moaned as she sank the last of his shaft inside her.

"Your wish is my command." With thumb and forefinger, Alex squeezed the taut peaks, increasing the pressure as she began to ride him.

"Harder." Her back arched with her demand, her breasts pressing deeper into his hands.

"Give me more."

"Alex."

"Faster, Sadie." He gave her nipples a hard tug. "Ride me."

And she did.

She took him deep on every plunge. Contracted around him on each slide up. They were both breathing hard now, their bodies slapping together faster and faster. Harder and harder.

He wasn't sure how long she rode him before it became too much. Not enough. Releasing her breasts, Alex gripped her ass cheeks and flipped them over, pinning her under him.

His hips pistoned back and forth, his cock driving into her over and over until she was calling out his name and coming around him.

Her climax shattered the last of his resistance and he came, buried to the balls, with a shout of pure pleasure.

He saw stars. Heard bells. Was sure he was floating somewhere near the ceiling looking down at the two of them sprawled in complete satisfaction.

She killed him.

Every time.

How did they keep getting better at this?

"Wow."

"Yeah. That about sums it up," he murmured into her neck.

He couldn't move. Knew he should because he had to be crushing her, except he didn't have the energy—or the brainpower—to manage it yet.

"I always think it can't be as good as I remember."

All he could do was nod.

"If this keeps up we'll kill each other."

Alex grinned. "Yeah. But what a way to go."

132

CHAPTER 26

"No, not that one, the Phillips head."

Sadie stared at the screwdriver in her hand and tried to figure out how she'd gotten it wrong. "You asked for a screwdriver."

"I asked for a Phillips head screwdriver." Alex glanced up from where he was holding the bed frame together. He studied her for several seconds before he smiled. "You don't know what I'm talking about, do you?"

"You wanted a screwdriver. This is a screwdriver." She held out the tool. "Isn't it?"

"Yes, but that's a flat-head screwdriver and I need a Phillips head."

"Um..." She looked into the toolbox on the floor beside her.

"It looks like a cross on the end."

"Oh!" Spotting the tool, she put the *flat-head* back and

picked up the *Phillips head*. "Here." She held it out with a grin.

"Look at you. We'll have you on a building site in no time," Alex said with a laugh.

"Ha! Not likely. You saw what I did to all this"—she waved her hand at the bed he almost had assembled in less than twenty minutes—"in a few hours. Imagine what I could do with days."

Laughing, he ducked his head and applied the screwdriver to something she couldn't see. "Good point. Maybe you should unpack another one of your boxes," he suggested. "I've got this from here."

She knew what he was doing. She'd dropped all the pieces he'd asked her to hold at least once while she'd played assistant. Sadie couldn't blame him. She wasn't exactly skilled in the handyman department. And if those skills were measured in negatives like numbers, she'd be firmly in the minus column.

Alex on the other hand, could probably manage anything he put his hands on. She grinned. He certainly managed her with them.

"Okay, I'll go finish the kitchen." Not that she had much, but she did want to get everything organized so she could start using it.

Eating takeaway when you lived in the city was completely different to doing it in a small town. For a start, most restaurants shut before eight on a weeknight, unlike Miami where you could get whatever you wanted twenty-four hours a day.

Leaving Alex to it, she went to the kitchen. There

were only two boxes left to unpack, which was good. What wasn't good was the contents of the four other boxes labeled kitchen that were piled on the counter tops. She'd put a few things in drawers, and her mugs were in the cupboard above the coffee maker she'd yet to plug in and use. Coffee was on her list for the grocery store.

First stop after the unpacking had to be the store. She needed more than just coffee. Other than some leftover pizza from her first night in Winter Lake, the fridge was empty. Nothing sat on the shelves in the pantry either. Protein bars and chocolate didn't count. She'd been living on both when she didn't go out for food the last few days.

She kept her notepad close and jotted down everything that came to mind as she slowly made her way through the piles on the counters and the final two boxes.

Closing the cupboard beside the oven, she smiled. It felt good to have everything away and how she wanted it. She had always shared a kitchen before and while she'd been able to make do, with her love of cooking, being able to have free rein would be so much better. Already ideas for meals were percolating in her head.

"Hey."

Turning she found Alex leaning against the counter that separated the kitchen area from the living space. "Hey. All done?"

"Yep. Wanna try it out?" He waggled his eyebrows at her.

"Didn't we already do that?"

"We tried out the mattress, not the frame." He moved

toward her, glancing at the neat counters. "Everything away?"

"Yes." She grinned. "Now I just have to get some food in here so I can cook."

He froze, his gaze returning to hers. "You cook?"

"Of course. Who can afford to eat out all the time when they've got student loans to pay off? It might be a thing for college students to live on ramen but I've never been a fan. Plus I worked in a restaurant part time right through school. I learned everything I could and most nights I talked the owner into letting me use the kitchen before I went home."

"This isn't much of a kitchen after what you're used to." He looked around, frowning. "Hell, that oven would barely fit a cake tin."

"Good thing I don't bake." With a smile she patted his cheek. "Don't worry, I once made Thanksgiving dinner with a two burner and a microwave."

"Really?"

Nodding, she moved into him and wrapped her arms around his waist. "Yes. Ask Mel next time she's revealing all my secrets to you."

Laughing he pulled her tight against him. "I'll be sure to do that."

Her stomach rumbled. All this talk of food obviously woke it up.

"Hungry?" he asked with an arch of one eyebrow. "Why don't we leave the rest of the unpacking for now and take that tour of town I promised you? I'll even throw in dinner at Della's Dina when we're done."

"It's not even lunch time. Don't you have to work?"

He'd mentioned being at work early this morning but he'd spent hours here and he hadn't taken a call or talked about leaving. And now that she thought about it, he'd rarely looked at his phone in all the time they'd been together.

"Nope. Being the boss has its perks. It also helps that I've got a trusted team working for me."

"And you don't have anything else you want to do?"

Patrick would have found any number of things to do besides spend time with her. She'd accepted it at the time. Hell, she'd been with him for four years and not once did she complain about his lack of attention, hadn't wanted to. Kind of explained why that relationship tanked.

"I have nothing to do except help you get settled here." He nodded at the boxes still in the living area. "And show you around town until you start work."

"That's not until Monday."

"I know." He kissed her quickly. "Now, let's go find something for lunch so we can start exploring Winter Lake."

"You can't take all this time off work to be with me."

Alex smiled as he let her go and brought his hands to her face. "Which part of 'I'm the boss' did you miss? As the boss, I can do whatever the hell I want."

"I feel bad about you missing work."

"Sadie, I'm not missing anything. I was already taking the week off. My crew knows what they're doing. If something important comes up and they need me, they'll call."

Frowning, she muttered, "Surely there's something better you could do than spend your time off with me."

"Jesus, woman. I *want* to be with you. I'd call in sick for a month if you promised to let me hang out with you."

"I'd bore you to death before we hit the second week."

"Doubtful. Now go get whatever you think you need for an afternoon out." He lowered his hands to her shoulders and spun her around. "I've got a spare jacket in the car if you don't have anything warm enough, and we'll stop at Winter Lake Wears at some point so you can see what they've got so you don't freeze your cute butt off when you head to work next week."

"I won't need a jacket at the office." Looking over her shoulder she frowned at him.

He slapped her ass. "Go. Get your bag or whatever and don't argue about the jacket. I'll go in and buy one without you if you keep arguing."

Sadie wasn't sure how she felt about that. Or the slap on her butt. It barely stung but she'd definitely felt it and the sensation that rolled through her along with the slight pain was something she'd have to think about later.

Right now she needed to grab her bag and shoes. Her stomach rumbled again. The cinnamon roll was long gone. Alex had only bought them one each. Not nearly enough to replenish the calories they'd burned while testing out her mattress.

A shiver slipped down her spine and burst into a ball of heat low in her pelvis.

They'd really tested that mattress. It had been at least an hour since they'd crawled off and started putting her bed together and yet she could still feel his hands on her. Her hands on him.

Maybe she could talk him into reissuing his invitation to test out the bedframe now he'd assembled it.

"No."

Eyes snapping to Alex, she tried to remove all expression from her face. "What?"

"You know what. Go. If we don't get out of here now, we're not leaving until we both have to go to work on Monday and that's not what I promised you." He moved away from her, toward the door. "Don't make me break that promise."

Did he want her that much? They'd spent the better part of the morning having sex, they should both be sated; he'd come twice and she'd lost count but was pretty sure he'd given her four orgasms.

"*Sadie.*"

Her name was a plea and while the idea of breaking his control was tempting, she really did want to see what Winter Lake had to offer and who better to show her around than a man who'd grown up here. A man she liked. A lot. Probably too much considering he was only supposed to be a one-night stand.

She'd screwed that up.

Then again, she'd been screwing things up from the start.

She'd planned on one night with Alec Dane and ended up with Alex Dean.

If she hadn't made that mistake, if she'd known who she was going home with that first night, would she have done it?

And if she hadn't, would she still be here, now, with Alex?

She had to think the answer to that was yes. Their chemistry was off the charts and neither of them seem to be able to keep their hands to themselves for very long.

When she'd dropped her towel earlier, she'd made the decision to continue having sex with Alex. But she'd secretly wanted more than that. She wanted to get to know Alex better, spend more time together outside her bedroom as well as in it.

She'd promised herself this move, this change of course in her life, would be about living, and while she hadn't planned on embarking on a new relationship it appeared as though she had no choice.

Alex wasn't backing away. He'd sought her out at every turn. He'd come after her when she'd fled that first morning and again when she'd left Miami.

After her experience with Patrick, she couldn't deny Alex's attention was exhilarating.

He'd said this thing between them was more than just sex but what did that really mean?

And was she brave enough to find out?

CHAPTER 27

"So where are we going again?" Sadie asked from the passenger seat of his truck.

He glanced over but quickly returned his gaze to the winding mountain road. "Broken Bay. It's a small town on the other side of the lake. It used to be the 'rich' end of town back in the days when logging was the business of the region."

"And we're going there because?"

"I want to check on my house."

From the corner of his eye, he saw her straighten. "I thought you lived in Winter Lake."

"I do. Now and before. But I bought one of the old lake front properties a year ago. I've spent months drawing up plans for the restoration. I've included a bunch of environmentally sustainable features while attempting to stay true to the original architecture. It'll take at least another month or so before it's finished."

"So you're going to move here when it's done?"

"That's the plan." He had another plan now. Convince Sadie to move in with him by then. He wanted her to love the place as much as he did.

"Hmm..."

He probably shouldn't have brought her over here. Except after he'd shown her around Winter Lake and they'd picked up a jacket suitable for mountain weather, he'd wanted her to see it. Needed her to see it. Needed to see her *in* it.

For the first time in his life he wanted to impress a woman and this house was his shining light. It showcased everything he stood for and had achieved. Everything he hoped to achieve yet.

Shit. He was thinking marriage and children and a home on the lake with a woman who wasn't even his girlfriend!

He was certainly putting the cart before the horse at the moment.

As much as he kept trying to reel himself in, to take slow steps or even step back, he couldn't seem to manage it.

Sadie hit him deep. Deeper than he would have thought possible before reconnecting with her in Miami.

He had to believe fate played a hand in them hooking up last Friday. In the plans Sadie had already made to move to Winter Lake.

He'd never been especially religious or superstitious or any of that mumbo-jumbo but he couldn't deny there was more than coincidence involved in them getting together.

So many things could easily have gone a different way starting with Alec being in town instead of out, and at the club with the rest of them on Friday night.

Rounding a bend in the road, he slowed the truck and pointed down to where Broken Bay could be seen hugging the edge of the lake below them.

"That's Broken Bay. There's only about a thousand people living here, on this side of the lake; the main population is in Winter Lake and the bay is really just an extension of Winter Lake. It's where all the 'monied' families lived during the logging boom."

"I read a bit about the logging in the area. It's no longer happening though, right?"

"No. It stopped years ago which is why a lot of the property in Broken Bay is rundown or even abandoned. No logging, no money. There's still a few of the older, richer families around. Harry Windburn, Winter Lake's mayor, is from here. His family is one of the area's founding ones," he explained as he drove down the mountain toward the water.

"Oh, I interviewed with him."

"He's a great guy. Does a lot for both towns. He owns Winter Lodge among other things. I'm pretty sure he owns a good deal of both towns as well as the old mill."

Harry had been a fixture in Winter Lake and Broken Bay for Alex's entire life. Harry had helped out when Alex's dad had died by giving his mother a job. She'd never worked before that and Alex had no doubt her life—and his—wouldn't have turned out as well without the man.

"He's saved a lot of people in this town."

"I liked him. He—" She sucked in a breath as he pulled the truck up in front of his place. "Holy shit! Is this your house!"

Peering through the windshield, he tried to look at the house from Sadie's point of view. Her awe didn't surprise him; he'd been equally enthralled when he'd first seen the place. She was a grand three-story beauty whose shine had dulled but was beginning to sparkle again.

What he wanted to know was if Sadie saw what he did when he looked at it. Did she see the potential?

"God. Living here would be amazing." She leaned forward, her hands on the dash, her nose right against the window. "I can see kids running around chasing a dog... Oh! Is that the lake?"

He smiled. "Yeah, the house is right on it. There's even a dock for a boat and jumping off."

"The kids would love that." Laughing she added, "The dog too."

She did see it. "Want to go inside?"

"Can we? Yes! Let's do that."

Before he could react, Sadie was out of the truck and racing for the front door. He wasn't worried about her going inside without him. The place might be a construction site but it was a safe one.

His men knew to keep things organized and she wasn't stupid. She wasn't about to pick up any tools or grab exposed wires.

Alex took his time following. Passing through the propped-open door, he stopped to listen to the sound of saws and drills hard at work. They were on the third floor finishing up the last of the renovations he'd designed.

He could hear Sadie talking to herself and headed in her direction. He smiled. Other than a few final touches and moving furniture in, the ground and second floors were done.

They'd finished this level first and he had planned to move in after he'd returned from Miami. The water and electricity had been switched back on after the final plumbing and electricals were hooked up while he was away.

Except now he wanted to wait.

He'd be lying if he said that decision had nothing to do with the woman currently oohing and ahhing over his kitchen. Pausing in the archway between the formal dining room and kitchen, he watched Sadie move from oven to fridge to pantry to sink back to the oven again.

"This is amazing. My mouth is watering just thinking about all the delicious food you'll cook in here."

"Not sure I'm the guy for that job."

She looked over at him, her hand caressing the stainless steel appliance in front of her. "What do you mean?"

"I can manage to put together an edible meal, but I'm pretty sure no one would call my efforts delicious." He shrugged. "They serve their purpose though."

Her mouth dropped open. Snapped shut. Shaking her head she looked around the room. "Why would you put in such a cook's kitchen if you can't really cook?"

He thought about her question. He had researched all the electrical appliances for their energy efficiency as well as their consumer ratings. He'd wanted the kitchen to serve two purposes.

One, it had to be practical as well as efficient.

And two, he believed the kitchen was the hub of a home, the center, the place where everyone came together, and he'd wanted his house to be a home.

"I may have to sneak in and cook from time to time. This place deserves to be used to the fullest." She grinned at him and winked. "Don't lock the back door."

"I'll give you a key." Words poured out before he thought them. "Or you could move in with me."

CHAPTER 28

I'll give you a key. Or you could move in with me.

Those two sentences had been playing on repeat in Sadie's head for weeks. The longer time marched on, the harder it got to ignore the desire to take Alex up on one of them. On both.

God. She was in love with the guy. So deep in love she couldn't remember what it was like to not feel him inside her heart.

She'd had such high hopes for her move to Winter Lake and every one of them had been blown right out of the water.

Her job was great, her co-workers super nice and from day one treated her like family. Hell, the whole town treated her like family.

She had no idea if that was because she was dating Alex or if it was how they'd be with any new arrival.

"Hey, Sadie, how are you?"

Sadie turned to see Carly and her sister Laura behind her in the checkout line. "Hi. Good. I'm good."

"All settled in?" Laura asked. "Not missing Miami?"

"Not even a little bit." She grinned. "Well, I miss Mel, but we talk on the phone every day and she's promised to come visit before the first snowfall so she doesn't have to wait a year to see me."

"Why would snow stop her from seeing you?" Carly asked.

"Because according to Mel, if she were meant to be around snow she'd have been born with a fur coat and considering she waxes any *fur* that might have the nerve to appear on her body, there isn't a chance in hell of her showing her face around here between the months of October and May," she explained.

"She sounds like our brother. He's gone soft since he moved south for college," Laura said.

"Hey, you going to Books and Bitches tonight?" Carly asked.

"Oh, is that tonight? I forgot." She glanced at her shopping cart. "I was planning a special meal for Alex…"

Carly held up a hand. "Say no more. I know you're anxious to get into that fabulous kitchen."

She'd been dying to use Alex's kitchen since the day he'd shown it to her. And today was the day.

It was move-in day.

Alex had spent all day moving his furniture, what he hadn't bought new and had delivered, from the rental he'd been living in these past months. Tonight they'd both sleep in the house over in Broken Bay. He'd insisted. Said he couldn't stay there the first night without her.

And if she were honest, she'd have to admit she didn't want him to stay there without her.

She wanted to live in that house.

She'd spent a hell of a lot of time and effort helping him furnish the place. It felt like hers—*theirs*—not just his.

"That's some serious thinking happening in there." Laura tapped her temple.

"Oh, sorry. It's been a crazy few weeks." It wasn't a lie. Between her new job, her new boyfriend, and all the new friends she made since moving to Winter Lake in July, Sadie's life had taken a swift turn to the right.

She'd gone from having zero social life where she spent most of her time between the pages of a book to being so busy she could count the number of books she'd read in the last two months on one hand. She was pretty sure that hadn't happened since before she could read.

"Well, you are dating Alex," Carly teased with a wink.

"Speaking of," Laura murmured.

"Hey, you just about done?" Alex's arms slid around her from behind. His lips pressed against her temple for a quick kiss.

"Yep."

"Good. I'm starved." His lips brushed her ear, his voice lowering to a whisper only she could hear. "And I see something I'm starving for." He nipped her lobe.

Heat rushed through her, clenching her sex and tightening her nipples.

"Good God, Alex, keep it PG in public. I'd hate to have to arrest you for lewd behavior," Laura complained.

Laughing, he pulled away and took control of the cart; moving it forward he began to unload her shopping on the belt. "Don't worry, Officer Murdock." He emphasized Laura's title even though she wasn't in uniform. "I'll be sure to keep my lewd behavior behind closed doors."

The wink he sent Sadie had her cheeks heating, her insides coiling tight. Damn. The man only had to look at her for her libido to kick into overdrive.

They'd gone at it from day one and didn't seem to be slowing down. And things had only gotten better. Which didn't seem possible because they'd been spectacular from the start.

"Jeez." Carly faked a gag. "You two make me sick."

Laura laughed. "Love is so gross when it involves your cousin."

Sadie froze when Alex's gaze darted to hers. She knew she was in love with him and she thought—hoped—he felt the same but neither of them had voiced the word.

They hadn't really discussed anything about their relationship since that day at Alex's house and he'd uttered those words she couldn't forget.

Clearing his throat, Alex turned to his cousins. "Yeah, gross. It's why I have to slap my hand over Nash's mouth whenever he starts talking about doing something with handcuffs—"

Laura slapped a hand over Alex's mouth. "Enough. I'm out of here."

She walked away, Carly following with an eye roll and a mouthed 'you're dead' aimed at Alex.

From what Sadie knew, Alex's construction manager and Laura had had a very public, very steamy encounter a few weeks back that she refused to talk about and he couldn't shut up about.

"C'mon." Alex grabbed her hand. "We've got a meal to make."

She smiled. He'd insisted if she was cooking, he'd be helping and she couldn't wait. "Are you sure you're up for the task?"

"With you? I'm up for anything. Everything."

She could read between the lines. She knew they'd just crossed a line courtesy of his cousin shoving them over but it didn't matter who'd put it out there. They had been there for weeks and whether they were in the line at the grocery store or in bed naked it was still there between them.

"I love you." The words were out of her mouth without thought and while a few hours ago, they might have made her panic, right now they didn't. Nothing about the way Alex made her feel made her panic. She wanted to take the next step in their relationship. Was more than ready to take it.

He pulled her close. "I love you too."

Pushing up to her toes, she pressed her mouth to his and spoke against his lips. "I want that key."

"Then you'll move in with me," he answered.

She laughed into his mouth. "Are we really doing this?"

"Yes." He wrapped his arms around her waist and picked her up. "We are so doing this. Actually, it's done."

She leaned her head back. "What do you mean it's done?"

"I moved your stuff into the house along with mine." He grinned.

"You... I..." She sucked in a breath and finally got her brain and mouth connected. "You moved me in? Without asking?"

"Like you could leave that kitchen after you'd cooked in it."

"Oh, I see, it's all about the kitchen, is it?"

"It's a great kitchen."

"It's the best kitchen."

"We should go home and give it some love before it feels neglected."

"We should."

"We can't let a day go by without showing it some love."

"No we can't." She grinned. They were no longer talking about a kitchen.

ALEX RUBBED his cold hands together. They'd had a snowfall last night. Not enough to really stick but definitely enough to make this evening more special for Sadie.

He patted his pocket. Checked he had the tickets for their time slot.

She should be home any second...

The front door opened and in walked the woman he'd finally convinced to move in with him. Okay, fine, he'd moved her things in so she couldn't argue. Not that she'd wanted to.

However it happened it had the same result. Her, in his bed and in his house. *Their* house.

They'd been living together for not quite two months and already he knew this was it for him.

Sadie was still a little more cautious. Wanted them to take it slower. And while he was okay with doing that, he didn't need to.

He'd already purchased the ring. He wouldn't give it to her yet though. No point starting another discussion on being sure—not rushing.

"Hey." She removed the scarf from around her neck. "You're home early."

"I've got a date." He grinned.

Her head snapped around, her wide eyes locking on his. "What?"

Alex walked over to her. "I've got a date."

"With w-who?"

He saw the panic in her eyes and cursed the fear and insecurity that sometimes grabbed hold of the woman he loved with all his heart.

Another reason to get his ring on her finger—and hers on his. An everyday reminder that she was his. He was hers. "With the woman of my dreams." Alex kissed her cold nose.

"Oh." The word left her mouth on a sigh.

"C'mon. You need to get changed." He wove their fingers together and led her up the stairs to their bedroom. "I've laid everything out. Don't ask any questions. I want it to be a surprise but I know how hard it is for you to keep that brain from working out puzzles, so if you think you know, don't say anything."

"Sounds intriguing."

"Nope. No intrigue here. Just us. Going out on a date." He stopped them near their bed. "Get changed. I'll be downstairs."

"Alex."

He turned back. "What?"

"I can't skate."

His mouth dropped open.

She shrugged. "You promised."

Alex grabbed both her hands. "You remember that?"

"Of course. And you never make a promise you don't keep."

He arched an eyebrow. "Really?"

Sadie nodded.

"So if I promise to love you forever, you'll believe me?"

"I do."

"Because... Wait. What?"

"I believe you."

"Then why the hell did it take so long to convince you to move in with me?"

"It wasn't exactly long and I needed to catch my breath."

"And did you? Catch your breath?"

"No." She shook her head. "It's seems feeling breathless twenty-four-seven is the new normal."

"Is that a good or bad thing?" God, he hoped it was good.

"Depends."

"On what?"

"If you feel the same."

"Sadie." Alex pulled her into his arms and held her tight. "You *are* my breath. The thought of being without you for one second leaves me unable to breathe at all."

"That doesn't sound good."

"It's not. It means you can't ever leave me." He tightened his arms.

"I'm not going anywhere."

Alex leaned back. For the first time in months he saw what he was looking for. She trusted their love. Was confident this was real—lasting. "Right. Stay right here."

Releasing her, Alex went to the walk-in closet and pulled open a drawer. The one that held the ties he rarely wore. Snatching up the small velvet-covered box, he headed back to where Sadie stood waiting.

"I wasn't going to do this yet. I've had it for weeks. I've known from almost the beginning." He dropped to one knee.

"Oh my God. What are you doing?"

"Sadie." He took her left hand in his right one. "I want you to wear something every day to remind you of my love. To remind you that even when I'm not there, my love surrounds you. Fills you."

She gasped when he popped the top of the box open to reveal a diamond solitaire set in gold.

"Will you do me the honor of becoming my wife?"

"Alex!"

He glanced up to find tears rolling down her cheeks. "We don't have to get married right away but I want to give you my promise to love you forever."

"Yes."

SADIE COULDN'T STOP LOOKING AT HER RING.

She still couldn't believe she wore it. They'd been together for only a few months but she knew.

She'd never love anyone the way she loved Alex.

He'd become her world so quickly. So completely.

"Put your glove back on before you get frostbite." Alex slipped his arms around her waist, rested his chin on her shoulder, and peered down at her hand.

"I just wanted another peek."

He kissed the side of her head. "You can look at it all day, every day for the rest of your life."

"Yeah, but there'll never be another day like today."

"Oh. Why's that?"

"Today's the first day. The only day you'll get down on one knee and give me the ring that represents your promise to love me forever."

"Well, when you put it like that..." He spun her around in his arms. "Let's go home and make love for the first time with you wearing your ring."

"You realize I'll never be naked in front of you again."

He reared back. "What?"

She held up her hand, flashed her ring. "I'll always wear this."

Alex laughed and gave her a squeeze. "*That* I'll accept."

"It's hard to believe we're here, isn't it?"

"In some ways yes. And some no." He let her go and gripped her hand, pulling her away from the ice she'd spent more time sitting on than skating on. "If you'd asked me before we met again if I'd be here, I'd have said no. But from the second I saw you in that club, I knew my life had changed."

"You don't regret how fast things have happened?"

"No. You?"

They sat on a bench to remove their skates. "No." She leaned over and kissed him.

"Mmm..." He reached down and unlaced her boots. "Let's get out of here so I can have more of those."

Sadie laughed.

"What's so funny?"

"You make me happy. Happier than I've ever been."

Alex chuckled, pulled her close, and stole another kiss before grinning at her. "And to think. It all started with a daring mistake."

"You know I don't think of it as a mistake. Not anymore." She cupped the hand with her ring around his jaw. "I'll always be grateful that I thought you were someone else because I don't think I would have had the courage to go home with you otherwise."

"Sadie—"

She placed her thumb over his lips. "No, let me finish. I may have thought you were someone else but Alex, I love you, who you are, the way you are. Everything about you is what I want, what I need, and I'll never regret the way we got together. Not for one second."

He pressed his lips to her thump in a hard kiss then spoke against it. "I love you the way you are too, *Dee*." he winked. "Now let's go home."

If you enjoyed this book, please consider leaving a review. It only takes a few minutes and you'll be helping other readers find stories they'll enjoy, as well as supporting authors you love.

For what's coming next, latest releases, sales and more, join
Rhian's Royal Readers
http://www.rhiancahill.com/contact/newsletter/

ACKNOWLEDGMENTS

I have to thank Carly Phillips. Without her the original version of Alex and Sadie's story would never have been told. Thank you for letting me play in your world for a little while.

I never would have stepped into Carly's world without Erin Nicholas pointing the way. Thanks for talking me into writing Sadie and Alex. And thank you for being a friend.

Fedora, once again you slap me into shape. Or is that sharp? ;) I know I push us both to the line a lot but I promise to do better next time.

I also want to thank every reader who has joined me on this new adventure. I'm humbled and thrilled that you pick up my books.

Thank you for taking a chance on characters who've been around a while. I hope you love the deeper look at them and the new characters popping up with each book in the Winter Lake series.

xoxo

Rhian

ABOUT THE AUTHOR

Rhian Cahill is the alter ego of a former stay-at-home mother of four. With motherly duties rapidly dwindling, Rhian is able to make use of the fertile imagination she used to keep herself sane for all those years of slavery. Years spent living overseas and visiting tropical climates have helped inspire some steamy stories.

Multi-published in erotic romance, paranormal romance, and contemporary romance, Rhian, with the help of Mr. Muse, spends her days and nights writing.

When not glued to the keyboard you'll find her, book or knitting in hand, avoiding any and all housework as much as possible.

For more on Rhian –

Website – http://www.rhiancahill.com/
Newsletter signup – http://www.rhiancahill.com/contact/newsletter/
FaceBook – https://www.facebook.com/RhianCahillAuthor

Instagram – http://instagram.com/rhiancahill/
Twitter – https://twitter.com/RhianCahill
BookBub – https://www.bookbub.com/authors/rhian-cahill
Goodreads – https://www.goodreads.com/rhian_cahill

WHEN YOU LOVE SOMEONE
WINTER LAKE BOOK 3

When it comes to love the tough guys always go down the hardest.

Sophie Collins is used to the adoring attention from her fans but the overzealous one who cooked her a meal and left it—with heating instructions—in her fridge has gone too far. No longer safe in her own house, she hops a plane and travels halfway around the world.

He was sent to bring her home safe. But from the minute Sophie falls into Stone's arms he knows she's not the only thing in danger. He's a hardened warrior trained to kill with his bare hands and one too sweet too young pop singer is bringing him to his knees.

If he can't keep her safe and neutralize the threat he stands to lose more than his client. He'll lose his heart.

Chapter 1

6am Saturday - Sydney, Australia

"Fuck. This guy has a serious hard-on for our girl."

Stone grunted in acknowledgement and glowered at the four walls boxing them in.

Every square inch—including the ceiling—was covered with photos of Sophie Collins.

She was a good-looking woman—hell, she was hot—and you couldn't hold it against a man for admiring the sexy songstress, but these pictures made Stone's gut churn and his blood boil.

This went beyond normal admiration. It wasn't the work of a besotted teenage boy or overzealous fan. What was spread out in front of them took this case from fanatical follower to obsessed stalker in the blink of an eye.

Something familiar snagged his gaze and he leaned in close for a better look. Recognition slammed into him. Sophie's bed. "Holy shit. He's got a feed into her house."

"What?" Ford Moreland charged over, shouldered him out of the way and bent to study the picture Stone pointed at. "Get someone in her fucking house right now, Aiden," his boss yelled. "I want whatever link this cock has shut down."

Stone liked working for Aiden and Ford Moreland. The brothers might be a little rough around the edges most of the time, but he appreciated that there was no beating around the bush, no bullshit, no sugar-coating. If a job needed doing, it got done ASAP.

Their company, Landlocked, dealt with all forms of security—high-tech systems for buildings, computer networks, etcetera—and Stone's favorite, and area of expertise: personal protection.

Except they hadn't done a great job of protecting Sophie Collins.

She was missing.

Twenty hours and counting since anyone had lain eyes on her.

Chip burst through the shed doorway behind them, laptop in hand. "You're not gonna like this, boss."

Ford laughed, the sound harsh and humorless as he turned to face the other man. "Yeah, 'cause I'm liking what I've seen so far." Blowing out a breath, he nodded. "Give it to me."

"He piggy-backed our system to get a visual inside her house. He also hijacked our trackers. That's why all the feeds went dead yesterday. I reactivated everything but nothing's pinging. Yet."

"Jesus fucking Christ. Who *is* this guy?" Ford growled. "I want a name and I want it *now*."

Stone knew how Ford felt. He'd wanted the guy's name a week ago when they thought they were dealing with nothing more than an overzealous fan.

If the fact the owner of this property, Henry Whittaker, appeared to be a ghost hadn't clued them in then the shed they stood in blew that notion to smithereens.

They'd either underestimated this guy or he'd escalated one thousand percent in the last week.

He hated to admit it, but they'd miscalculated. They

weren't dealing with a simple fan gone rogue—they never had been.

They had to get a handle on the situation. Fast.

The bastard had dodged them at every turn though. Hell, the fucker had not only gotten inside Sophie's house on their watch, he'd stuck around long enough to make himself a meal, for Christ's sake.

Even left a plate with reheating instructions—among other *gifts*—for Sophie, all while avoiding being caught on camera.

In the last twenty hours, everything had gone pear-shaped. Their client was missing and their target seemed to be the invisible man. He couldn't remember a more FUBAR job.

If they didn't find Sophie soon, he feared this guy would—if he hadn't already—and Stone didn't think the prick had anything pleasant planned for the pretty pop star.

The only thing they had going in their favor was Sophie had left her house alone. She appeared rushed and a little freaked out but she'd definitely been by herself when Land-locked's security cameras taped her lugging a suitcase through her front door.

But with her location still unknown they couldn't protect her, and with the evidence in front of them Stone had to acknowledge she needed their protection far more than any of them had thought.

"Any intel on where she is now?" Stone asked. If anyone could track the un-trackable, it was Chip.

"I might have the answer to that." Aiden strode into

the shed, eyes focused on the tablet in his hand. "But Ford isn't gonna like it."

Ford snorted. "Oh, yeah, because Ford's in love with every damn fucking thing so far."

Stone's lips twitched. His boss always managed to put a smile on his face in spite of whatever shit-hole they found themselves in. Ford's warped sense of humor had saved their sanity on more than one job over the years.

"First, this guy isn't as smart as we think. Jack's grabbing the genius behind the hacking now," Aiden offered.

"For fuck's sake," Stone cursed. This shit just kept getting better and better. "There are *two* people involved?"

"Explain," Ford growled over Stone's words.

"Give me a sec..." Aiden tapped away.

Stone was on the verge of grabbing his boss by the throat when Aiden spoke again.

"Ah, there. Sophie Collins hopped a plane for LA about four hours after we lost her. Here's the part you're *really* not going to like."

Stone had had enough. "Cut the BS and spit it out!"

His temples throbbed and his jaw ached from grinding his back teeth. He hated feeling useless and right now he felt downright impotent.

They needed to find Sophie Collins *now*.

"According to our perp's email he boarded the same aircraft under the name Henry Whittaker."

"He was on her fucking plane?" Stone exploded. The pounding in his head a moment ago was nothing compared to the thunder roaring through him now. How could they have screwed the situation up so badly?

"Easy there." Ford gripped Stone's shoulder, digging his fingers in hard, no doubt to keep him in place. Satisfied Stone wasn't going anywhere, Ford nodded at his brother. "What else, Aiden?"

Aiden eyed Stone for a moment, one eyebrow cocked, before returning his gaze to the information in front of him. "I'm still following the trail but Sophie hired a limo to take her to The Beverly Hilton. She's booked in for a two-week stay. Can't find Henry Whittaker on the guest register."

"How did this non-existent Henry Whittaker get a passport?" Ford aimed the question at Chip. "I want everything you find on this guy and I don't care how you get the information."

Chip nodded and began furiously tapping at the keys of his ever-present laptop.

A gangly teenager—all of sixteen, judging by the fuzz on his chin—stumbled into the shed.

Jack calmly strolled in behind him. "Got the little shit. Had to drag his ass out of bed."

The "little shit" glanced around, eyes widening with each man his gaze landed on. His prominent Adam's apple bobbed up and down his skinny neck as he swallowed.

When he spotted the photos covering the walls, his mouth dropped open and his eyes almost bugged right out of his head. "What the...?" He spun toward the door.

"Whoa." Jack grabbed the waistband of the kid's pants and swung him back around. "Stay right where you are. We are not done."

"But..." The kid's terrified gaze pinged around the room, avoiding eye contact with the men surrounding him.

"What's your name?" Ford asked in a mild tone, but Stone could hear the rage—the urgency—vibrating in each word.

"M-Mike." The kid licked his lips. "I d-don't know anything about t-this. I j-just did what he p-paid me for."

Not bothering to modulate his anger the way his brother had, Aiden stepped forward, got right in the kid's face and demanded, "Who and what?"

"G-G-G-George." The kid hooked a thumb over his shoulder toward the house visible through the busted-off-its-hinges shed door behind him. "H-he lives here."

Aiden arched an eyebrow. "George?"

"Y-yeah." The kid nodded, his Adam's apple bobbing several times, sweat beading on his forehead and upper lip.

"Got a last name?" Ford asked.

"D-D-D-Davis," the kid sputtered.

Stone couldn't decide if the stammering was nerves or a genuine affliction.

Not that it mattered. He didn't care about the kid beyond what he could tell them about Sophie's mysterious stalker.

It chapped Stone's ass to think this kid probably knew more about the guy than they did. Including what he looked like. So far they had three descriptions of Whittaker. If that was even his name.

"How many fucking names does this prick have?" Stone barked, the question aimed at no one in particular.

He could hear his frustration leaching into his voice

and tried to rein in his temper but feared he was fighting a losing battle; with every second his annoyance at the situation escalated.

"I've got a bead on five…" Chip murmured as he tapped away on his laptop.

"Five?" Stone asked in disbelief.

"It's irrelevant." Ford turned and faced Stone head-on. "Get on the first flight to LA. Find Sophie. Bring her home. Find Henry/George/whoever-the-fuck-he-is today. If he's touched her, he doesn't take another breath."

Stone's spine snapped straight, his whole body going rigid. He didn't think Ford meant for him to actually terminate the guy. Not really. But he completely understood the seriousness of his boss's words.

This guy would pay for anything and everything he'd done to Sophie Collins.

And it wasn't as though Stone couldn't put the guy down if necessary. He'd been given kill orders before. And while he'd done his job back then, followed every order to the letter, he'd never once felt the pleasure currently flowing through his veins at the thought of taking someone out.

He'd do his job. Find this guy and take him down.

For Sophie.

"Don't worry, boss. The motherfucker is going down. Hard."

Independent, career-minded Melinda Shaw has singlehandedly built one of Miami's premier event-management companies, but success hasn't stopped her heart from shifting its focus to marriage and children. Still, she's not about to burden a younger man with her fantasies of familial grandeur...until she does.

Their combustible sexual chemistry notwithstanding, Grady still has to work overtime to convince Mel he wants her despite their impending parenthood, not because of it. It'll take almost losing everything—and more than a few of Grady's famous moves—to score Mel's heart once and for all.

Wild Rush Of Love

Drinks aren't the only thing this barman is serving up.

Tending bar at Winter Lake Lodge, Rush Whelan enjoys all the fun with the female clientele, with none of the commitment. They come for vacation—and for Rush, in his bed—then they go. Until Sabreena. After spending her entire holiday together, Rush still can't get the shy beauty out of his mind. When he finds himself with some unexpected time off, there's only one thing to do—follow Reena home.

Waitress Sabreena Howe is grateful for the built-in family that comes with working at Pat's Pub. Mr. Collins and his brood have taken in more than a few strays, Reena among them. But even with their support, Reena has trouble letting people get close... including Rush. Despite their instant connection, Reena allowed fear to abort what could have been their amazing last night together.

When Rush shows up in Baltimore, Reena finally sets her trepidation aside, exploring her newfound sensuality even though she suspects another brief week together can only lead to heartbreak. Her home is here; Rush's is hundreds of miles away.

But the heart knows no time or distance. If Reena can redefine her definition of home, she'll find love is the greatest wild rush of all.

Hearts Are Wild Series

No More Talking (novella)

Dare You To (novella)

Mad Love

Boys Of Summer

Bondi Beach Boys

Sand, Surf And Sunnie

Only You Series

All Of You

Holiday Romances

Christmas Wishes

New Year's Kisses

Valentine's Dates

Secret Santa

Frosty's Snowmen Series

A Touch Of Frost

A Kiss From Kringle

A Taste For Kandy

Secret Confessions

Sydney Housewives – Virginia

Standalone Titles

Make You Burn

PARANORMAL ROMANCE

Coyote Hunger Series

Coyote Home

Coyote Wild

Coyote Whispers

Coyote Law (novella)

Coyote Lies

For a full list of available books visit

http://www.rhiancahill.com/books/

For what's coming next, latest releases, sales and more, join

Rhian's Royal Readers

http://www.rhiancahill.com/contact/newsletter/

www.ingramcontent.com/pod-product-compliance
Lightning Source LLC
Chambersburg PA
CBHW030800190726
48285CB00003B/954